HIS TO LEARN

Sons of Sicily - Book One

SKYLAR WEST

Published by Blushing Books
An Imprint of
ABCD Graphics and Design, Inc.
A Virginia Corporation
977 Seminole Trail #233
Charlottesville, VA 22901

©2021
All rights reserved.

Skylar West
His to Learn

eBook ISBN: 978-1-64563-061-6
Print ISBN: 978-1-64563-771-4
v6

Cover Art by ABCD Graphics & Design
This book contains fantasy themes appropriate for mature readers only.
Nothing in this book should be interpreted as Blushing Books' or
the author's advocating any non-consensual sexual activity.

Prologue

Theresa

As I pulled up in front of the Falcone mansion, my stomach churned. Attending the wake was a mistake. My instincts told me to peel away from the extensive driveway and head for the safety of home. But the questions that have plagued me since I read of Maria Falcone's death needed assuaging, the foremost playing like a litany of bad music in my head. What if he had moved on without me and all that was left to share was the past?

I told myself to get a grip as my feelings were secondary to my purpose in being at the Falcone mansion. That was a half-truth; I was there for him. I put my car in park, joining the others littering the circular driveway. As I walked up the stone steps, I sighed in surrender. Maria Falcone, the only mother I had ever known, had died. I was here to pay my respects, to say goodbye. Maybe I wouldn't see Jimmy; maybe I was getting myself worked up for nothing.

My stomach roiled at the idea of seeing him as a man, seeing what he had become. I feared what I wanted most and

1

found myself wavering between my desire to see him and hoping to make a clean exit without seeing him. If I didn't see him, could I push Jimmy Falcone into the recesses of my childhood and pull him out as a fond memory when I needed one.

But even as that thought crested, I knew it was a lie. The ache I felt for Jimmy was not something that would ever go away; it was as permanent as his handprint was all those years ago. Standing on the threshold of the entrance, I tugged my black mini skirt and flicked my hair into place. I reached out my trembling hand for the door handle, and taking a deep breath, I pulled it open and stepped inside.

The great hall of the mansion was filled to capacity for Maria's wake. My social anxiety reared its head at the size of the crowd. Upon further inspection, I noticed the room was predominantly filled with family, and that did not help the urge to flee. Until something else hit me that was just as powerful—the sense that I was being watched.

I stood still, my eyes roving around the room, and then I saw him. The shock to my body was beyond what I could have fabricated based on my memories of Jimmy. My breath hitched and my legs trembled. His tall, over six-foot frame was clear now from the other side of the room. He stared at me so intently that I wondered if I was naked—I certainly felt as though I was.

In a room of Italians with an average height of five foot five inches, Jimmy looked like a runway model. He was gorgeous. His eyes held a predatory gleam. I watched him excuse himself without ever taking his eyes off me.

He stalked toward me, every inch of his form and energy screaming dominant. I realized that my desires were way beyond my comfort zone. Unconsciously, I started to back away, until my butt banged into the door behind me. Oh, my God, my lady parts clenched as he made his way over to me.

Then he was there and stopped directly in front of me. I held my breath.

"Theresa." He looked me up and down. "Look at you, all grown up."

"Um, hi, Jimmy."

He grabbed my arm without another word and stalked away from the crowd, bringing me into what I assumed was his office, tucked out of the way and very private. He pointed at a comfortable wingback while he takes the office chair behind his desk, clearly making a power play.

I giggled nervously and said, "This reminds me of the principal's office at school. I'm not in trouble already, am I?"

His eyes glittered dangerously. "Do you want to be in trouble, Theresa?"

Damn, the way he drew out my name when he said it had my body sizzling with lust. I felt my chest heave as I sought the oxygen that just got sucked out of my body when he made my lady parts clench. Thank God I was sitting as I couldn't imagine my legs effectively holding me up. Needing to ground myself, I shifted my gaze from him to the window behind his head. A young girl of maybe twelve who looks an awful lot like Jimmy was standing outside. My stomach flip-flopped. He had a daughter; I should leave.

"Is that your daughter?"

Jimmy turned his head, his expression quickly shifted from predator to displeasure. "Stay here," he ordered. I wanted to flip him off, but something made me acquiescent. A moment later, I saw Jimmy with his daughter. He whispered something in her ear, and she adamantly shook her head in response. He gave her jean-clad bottom a smack and then quickly pulled her in for a hug.

She buried her face in his chest as he wrapped his strong arms around her. I could see his lips still moving, but I had no idea what he was saying. When she pulled away, she was wearing a huge smile. I guess whatever he said to her must have been encouraging. She skipped away, both disappearing from my sight line.

The domestic scene I just witnessed trigged a memory—Jimmy and I were hanging out in the treehouse he and his father built for us when we were kids. The memory was based off a habitual scene we played out together hundreds of times, 'house.'

My mind traveled back to the treehouse, the last time we were in it, just before the Falcone family moved. Jimmy suddenly said, "Wife! Where are my slippers and pipe?"

He'd just shared with me that his family was moving. I was really upset, and he was trying to take my mind off it by playing our old game. But instead of making me laugh, as intended, I got pissed off and answered, "Go fuck yourself, Jimmy, I want a divorce." I don't know who had been more shocked, him or me. Then I started laughing hard, like a crazy person.

Jimmy hadn't thought it funny. He sat down on the only chair in the clubhouse and pulled me over his lap. He pushed my head toward the plank floor so my ass was right in his face. I'd felt so humiliated, but also a little excited. To hide the fact, I had started kicking and he started spanking.

"What the hell, Jimmy? It was a joke, now let me go." When my words didn't dissuade him, I tried again, "I swear to God, Jimmy, when I get up, I'm going to—"

"What, Theresa, what are you going to do, hit me with your little girly fists? Don't you ever say the divorce word to me, Theresa Romano, because it won't happen. You're mine." He punctuated each word with a hard smack to my ass.

"Jimmy, it's a game; we're just goofing off." His answer was to continue to rain blows down on my unprotected ass. "Stop, please, let me up."

"No."

4

Now I was mad, the increasing sting in my backside making me angrier with each crack. "You bastard," I hissed, renewing my efforts. "Let me up this instant."

"Oh, ho, ho! You think it's okay to swear at me, little girl? You're staying over my lap until you beg."

I was so engrossed in the memory, I startled when Jimmy perched himself against the edge of the desk, mere inches away from where I was sitting, bringing me abruptly back to the present. My gaze traveled up his chiseled body and rested on his chest. I felt his eyes bearing down on me, too intense for me to investigate, especially after what I'd been remembering about us.

Embarrassment created a heat that bloomed on my chest and quickly spread to my face. Gathering my courage, I allowed my gaze to travel up to Jimmy's face. His expression reflected sardonic amusement.

"Blush is such a becoming color on you, Theresa," he said, the meaning of his words clear as his predatory gaze turned into a leer. My blush deepened.

"I bet I can guess what you're remembering right now." He leaned forward and reached out his hand to cup my chin. I tried not to moan at the contact. Jimmy's hand was sending bolts of lightning through me as he ran his fingers gently over my jaw.

"Why are you here, Theresa, why did you come?" he asked. His voice was so sexy my nether region slipped into fast forward. His eyes held me captive, waiting for a response as every nerve in my body was alive and my parts were on fire.

"B-because," I stuttered. "Because I want to pay my respects to your mother; you know she meant a lot to me." My voice hiked a bit at the end, my purpose for being there lending strength to my words. At least enough to break the temporary control that Jimmy was easily exuding over me.

"Why did you bring me in here?" I countered, coming

back in control of my faculties. He sighed and dropped his hand from my chin.

"Let's go see the family." He wrapped my arm around his and we left his office.

I was unaware of exactly what business practices the family was invested in to have amassed, what clearly must have been, a large fortune. Looking around, I could see my and Jimmy's childhood homes fitting inside this monstrosity at least five times. I chanced to peek at him from beneath my lashes. The man was at home with his wealth, belonging to this large lifestyle he had created.

Jimmy's daughter walked down the spiral staircase toward us, now dressed in a black satin dress with ballet flats. Her long tresses are pulled back in a French braid. I glanced at Jimmy; he wore a smile of approval at her appearance. In response, her face lit up until she glanced at me on her father's arm. I watched her expression change to hostility.

"Daddy?" She stopped on the last stair and lifted her chin as she gazed down at me in an attempt to intimidate. How I admired her spunk.

"Maggie," Jimmy said, drawing her down the last stair and into his other arm. "This is my childhood best friend, Theresa. And this beautiful young woman is my princess, Maggie."

"*The* Theresa?" Her eyes grew round. "Finally," she squealed, stepping out of her father's arm and into mine. "I have been like wanting to meet you for like ever."

Maggie's big eyes and cute dimples were so disarming, I couldn't help falling in love with her on the spot. "Well, I am very happy to meet you too, Princess Maggie," I said enthusiastically. She beamed at me before pulling away from our awkward one arm embrace.

A crash from the kitchen startled us. "Excuse me, ladies. I see I'm needed. Mags, please show Theresa around while I'm gone, principessa."

"Yes, Daddy," she agreed as he kissed her cheek. Then Jimmy disappeared through the double doors leading to what I assumed was the kitchen.

"How long have you known my dad?"

"Mmm, since forever. Jimmy was two when I was born. We lived next door to each other until the family moved here when he was fifteen." We took our time moving about the room. Maggie seemed more interested in steering me than in introducing me. I was good with that; just being there stressed me out. I didn't need to add to it with unnecessary introductions.

"Maggie, how did you hear about me? Was it through your dad?"

She shook her head no. "Nonna—she used to tell me stories about you and my dad. She told me that I reminded her of you. She said you were tough and sweet, and that is why daddy and you were besties."

I want to ask more, but Maggie brought us to a stop in front of a dense group of men, all of whom seemed vaguely familiar. As they parted, I saw James Senior in the center of the group. He appeared startled to see me.

"Theresa." He pulled me in, planting a kiss on either cheek. "Let me look at you." He held me at arm's length. I knew my five-foot-five frame showed well as I was in good shape. I was a runner, so my legs were shapely and on display in the short skirt I'd chosen.

I admit, that while I was choosing my outfit, I imagined Jimmy salivating over my legs. I added a matching jacket to the form-fitting mini skirt and black wedge heels to accentuate my ankles. James Senior clucked his tongue.

"You're too skinny, Bella."

I laughed. "James, you would think a woman weighing in at two hundred pounds was too skinny."

He chuckled. "Have you seen Jimmy?"

I nodded. "Yes, but I'm not here for him." I was such a liar. "I'm here to see you and the family and give my condolences. I loved Maria like a mother, you know that. In fact, she was the only mother I ever knew."

He averted his gaze as he nodded in agreement with my words. He was hurting, so I gave him a hug and then allowed Maggie to move us along. We stopped at a group of women, all looking to be around age twenty. It was hard not to grimace as they spoke, as the stories were way to graphic for a twelve-year-old. I moved us along and asked, "Maggie, is your mother in attendance? If so, I would love to meet her."

She shook her head. "She died just before I turned one. I don't remember her."

I felt like a schmuck. I should have asked Jimmy, prior to asking her. "I'm so sorry, Maggie," I said as I reached for her hand, holding it between both of mine. "I guess your grandmother was your world?" She nodded, her eyes heavy with unshed tears.

"I lost my mother when I was a baby, too, just like you. And for a long time, your grandmother was like my mother. Jimmy and I, well, we were besties growing up because I was always at the Falcone house. My dad worked hard so we could keep our house, and I have no other family."

I reached out for her other hand and held them both in mine. "I am truly sorry, Maggie, for your loss." A large tear that had been hovering finally fell and rolled down her porcelain cheek. I let go of one of her hands and wiped it away and then pulled her in for a hug.

"It will be okay, Maggie," I crooned. "Let it all out, darling." And with my words, the dam unleashed. A few minutes later, Jimmy came around the corner and stopped so abruptly that he slid on the Italian marble flooring and landed on his ass by our feet.

Our moment of grieving was over and replaced with

laughter as Maggie and I gazed down at Jimmy. His quick succession of changing facial expressions had Maggie and me in peals of laughter until his resting face morphed into a man with a plan.

"So, you girls think me landing on my ass is funny, do you? We'll see how funny you think it is when I catch you."

Yay, a game, my inner goddess clapped. Maggie and I ran screeching away, down one wing, and out into the backyard. Jimmy followed, making monster sounds as he chased us. We giggled in anticipation of being grabbed by the monster. This was just like when we were kids, except now, I was hobbled by my heels. "Help," I screeched as Jimmy caught me.

"Maggie," he growled. "I caught your friend. What should I do, eat her?"

I pretended mock fear of being eaten.

Maggie popped her head out from behind a rose bush. "Kiss her, Daddy."

Jimmy pulled me in tight and kissed me. Not a peck as I had expected, but a deep kiss, his tongue opening my lips, commanding, dominating, drinking deeply. My eyes flew open at the invasion. His were already open, the predatory look in his eyes sealing my future. I tried pulling away, wanting - no needing - to escape from him.

Maggie tapped him on the shoulder. "That's quite the kiss, Dad."

Jimmy looked up, stunned, his lips finally releasing me.

Maggie and I laughed again at his expense as we sauntered away, but not before he swatted my ass. It was light, but it seared me with heat. Everything about Jimmy Falcone spoke of possession. If I weren't careful, I would be his next acquisition.

Jimmy left us then to go and speak with more guests that have arrived during our romp outside. I said my goodbyes to

Maggie and James Senior and headed for the door, hoping to escape before Jimmy noticed me leaving.

I scanned the extensive u-shaped driveway for my car. The new guests had blocked me in. Crap! So much for a clean escape. I took a breath. *Calm down, Theresa,* I coaxed myself. How could I get out of this situation without talking to Jimmy? Being in his presence had set off my lady parts that I'd been purposely keeping shut off for a few years. I hadn't dated since college, and I didn't want to start now. That last experience with Steve had been humiliating and had put me off men.

I remembered I had a change of clothes in my trunk and running shoes. Oh, hurray! I could do this. I got my items from the trunk and snuck down the side of the house, ducking behind a sculptured bush.

I pulled off my wedges and wiggled out of my skirt and jacket. I was in my camisole and G-string when Jimmy and another guy come around the corner. I don't know who was more surprised, them or me. I hugged my clothing to the front of my body in a vain attempt at covering up. Jimmy walked straight to me while taking off his suit coat and covered me up.

"Give me a moment, Al."

"Sure, boss." Al continued around to the backyard.

"Theresa, what the hell are you doing, trying to give the wake an eyeful?"

I was thoroughly embarrassed. "Um, well, uh, you see, I need to leave, but my car is blocked by the new arrivals, so I grabbed a change of clothes so I could, you know, change, and then jog home. I figured I'd get the car later." I had been staring at the ground during this exchange.

Jimmy lifted my chin, gazing into my eyes. "Theresa, that doesn't explain why you are outside, instead of inside in a bathroom. Why didn't you tell me? I would have retrieved your car."

I tried to look away, but he wouldn't let me.

"Theresa," he growled. "I'm waiting for an answer."

"Um…" I trailed off.

"Geez Louise, woman, it's like being kids again. Do you need me to treat you like a kid, Theresa? Will that get your tongue wagging?" His threat did the trick.

"I'll have you know, James Junior, that I don't need anything or anyone. I was simply being polite and trying to not interrupt the wake."

"I think that you're lying to me, Tesoro. Try again. I warn you, if you lie to me, you'll have another trip down memory lane, only this one facing the ground as you dangle over my knee."

He pulled me closer, close enough that I could smell his scent—Italian coffee, aftershave, and man. Jimmy's scent was so masculine, my lady parts clenched in response.

"Um, well."

He marches over to a large garden boulder and put his foot on top. He was about to pull me over his knee. "Wait, Jimmy, please don't do that."

"Then the truth, amoré."

"I was afraid." My gaze moved from his face to the ground at my feet. "I was afraid of what I might find when I arrived. I was afraid that you had forgotten me or didn't care about me anymore. I was afraid you were happily married. But now I see you remember…many things. I needed to get away, fast. That's why I didn't say goodbye to you. That's why I was changing here, honest."

He took his foot off the boulder and pulled me into an embrace. "Good girl," he crooned. My physical response was at odds with my thoughts. I wanted to tell him to screw off.

My senses, however, were very much enjoying the embrace, and truth be told, being called a good girl was nice, too.

Finally, logic prevailed. "I must go, Jimmy. Do you think you can get my car unblocked?"

"Already done, little girl."

"Wait, what? And stop calling me that."

He chuckled. "I saw your dilemma and you sneaking down the side of the house. Al went to deal with it. You can go now." He stepped away from me in dismissal. I threw on my sports clothes and picked up my suit and heels. I stalked away when I heard, "I'll see you later, Tesoro."

I didn't respond, just kept walking until I arrived at my car. I got in and finally made my escape.

Chapter 1

Jimmy

It was eight days since I saw Theresa at my mother's wake. I'll never forget the way I felt when I looked up from talking to my mother's aunt, who had flown in from Sicily, and saw Theresa standing on the threshold of my house. She looked very unsure of herself and incredibly sexy. She oozed submissive energy that sent a pulse right down to my cock. Her curvy, athletic body begged for sex and plenty of it. My cock wanted me to drag her upstairs to my room and fuck her for days.

She hadn't grown much in height, maybe an inch or two since I last saw her. Her legs were long, strong, and made to be wrapped around me. Her round ass was full and looked firm, made for my hands to spank it. Her breasts were not large, but they were perky and begged to be pinched, caressed, kissed. Her auburn hair shone in the light from the stained-glass door. I watched her; she looked downright uncomfortable, but then she always did in crowds.

As I stalked toward her, my thoughts drifted to my childhood, which was filled with her. We'd gotten into trouble all the time, once throwing rocks at cars while hiding in trees. When our hiding spot was discovered, I'd told her to run. I got caught and took the belting from my pops. I didn't have a birthday memory without her in it or any memory I valued. She was my past; she had been everything.

We moved when I was fifteen, to the mansion where I still reside. Theresa visited me here once, right after the move. But things weren't the same. She seemed sad, and I was excited about my new life, new school, new challenges. Back then, the norm for me would have been to not let her leave until I knew what was bothering her, and then I would fix it. As my bestie, I would have done anything for her. But the move and the increase in social status had me focused on the future, not on Theresa, who represented the old hood.

We had chemistry, although we didn't know it at the time. Everything I found adorable about her as a little girl made me horny as a teenager. In many ways, my father's construction company taking off had come at the perfect time. I probably would have had her pregnant by graduation and married the next day. That was not the life I wanted for her.

Instead, I met Christine at a party one night. Our grade eleven one-night stand led to her being pregnant. Neither Christine nor I were interested in being parents in high school but were from Catholic families and abortion wasn't an option. But I have thanked God every day for bringing me Maggie, my princess, and the love of my life. She forced me to grow up fast. Especially after her mother and her mother's boyfriend died in a car accident after graduation when Maggie was only a year old.

Seeing Theresa at my mother's wake did all kinds of things to me. I think I felt compelled to play a game of monster with her and Maggie to do a reset. She wanted me. I could see that. I wanted her, too, only I was better at hiding it.

I wanted to touch her so badly, take her, own her, and make her scream my name over and over as I gave her orgasms she didn't even know were possible.

I'd marked her when I was young as my future mate, before the family moved. That was the real reason for the spanking in the treehouse. 'T' was mine from that moment, and the wake confirmed it. Based on her reaction to me with Maggie, I'd say she remembered that day, even if she didn't understand the ramifications of what it meant.

I'd almost come undone when I saw her semi-naked down by the side of my house. All I could think of was pushing her down on all fours and slipping inside her silky folds. Dismissing her was my way of getting a hold of myself. I knew she had been turned on, but she was also skittish. Letting her go was part of a bigger plan. Now that she was back in my life, my goal was to keep her in it.

"Jimmy!"

I shifted my focus back to the present in time to alter my stance and hit the soccer ball that was flying toward my face, into the net, scoring the winning goal. I kissed both sets of the index and middle fingers before extending them, just like my favorite soccer player, Claudio Marchisio. With the game over, I headed off the field and toward my car.

"Jimmy, where are you going?"

"Home; I'm a family man, remember."

"Come on, Jimmy, Maggie's almost thirteen; she doesn't want to hang out with her dad. Come out and have a few beers with us."

Maybe they were right; I'd been keeping a very close watch on Maggie. She had been very upset by the news of my mother's imminent death and, until the wake, very sad and shut down. The wake was a tipping point for her. What the magic ingredient was I didn't know. It could have been that the wake signified an ending and a beginning.

Her nonna—and surrogate mother—was gone. Theresa stepped in and was able to help Maggie grieve in a way I hadn't been able to. These could have just been fanciful thoughts; she was young, after all, and kids bounced back way faster than adults. It was easier to move on when you had your entire life ahead of you. Maybe an afternoon drinking beer with the guys would be okay.

"Sure. Okay, let's go," I finally conceded. Leaving my car parked, I piled into Al's 4 by 4 with the rest of the guys. We'd only driven a block, when Al slowed down.

"Would you look at that piece of ass," Al said as we passed the soccer field adjacent to the football field. I was in the back, on the passenger side, and couldn't see whom they were staring at.

"Oh, man, look at the way she bends. I'd love to plant my dick in her," Freddy moaned.

"In who," I asked?

"Look, boss." Al pulled over. There, standing in the center of the oval field was a woman with a gorgeous ass. We had a perfect view of it as she bent in half stretching her hamstrings. I felt like an idiot sitting at the side of the field with four other guys, staring. I was happy she was facing away so she couldn't see the five of us gawking at her. She stood up and, reaching back, pulled her foot to her amazing ass to stretch her quadriceps. Something looked strangely familiar about her.

When she turned to face us, I slunk down in my seat and moaned.

"Stop gawking," I shouted. Damn, it was Theresa, in her little shorty shorts. *Is that what she wears when she works out? How is it the silly woman hasn't been raped?* I was annoyed that her juicy ass was on display for anyone to see. "Drive around the park, Al, to where the cars are parked, by the bleachers."

Theresa

It was my workout day at the track and I'd just finished my routine and cool down. A few more stretches and I would head home and get ready for drinks with Robert. Today had been hard to focus on my workout. My thoughts constantly strayed to Jimmy Falcone. Eight days since the wake at his home and my lady parts were still squeezing when I pictured that wolfish grin of his. Absently, I reached behind to grab my foot as I bent my knee, drawing my toes toward my ass, getting a nice quad stretch.

I turned toward the parking lot as I lowered into a half squat with one leg extended to target my inner thigh for a good stretch. I noticed a man walking toward me at a rapid pace. He looked like Jimmy. As he got closer, I realized it *was* Jimmy. Shit, what was he doing here, and why did he look angry?

I quickly gazed around to see if there was anyone else out here that he could be stomping toward, but I was the only person on the field. The closer he got, the more I thought I should run. His aggressive gait, his glinting eyes, told me I was in trouble and… wait a second, I wasn't in trouble. I was single; I didn't owe him any sort of allegiance, and he certainly had no right to me, sexual or otherwise.

Still trying to convince myself of my independence, I turned to flee as he got within a few feet. "Theresa, stop!" I immediately stopped running and let him catch up to me. He grabbed my arm and, without a word, marched me over to the parking lot.

"Jimmy, what the hell? What's your problem?"

But he didn't answer, just wore a permanent scowl on his face as he continued to march, dragging me along with him. We were almost to the bleachers when I dug in my heels. "Get your goddamn hands off me. You are such an egotistical shithead!" His eyes grew round at the insult. Instead of continuing to drag me, as I'd expected, he picked me up and threw me over his shoulder.

"Keep quiet, little girl; one more comment out of you, and I'll tan your hide."

I stopped struggling. He was more than capable of doing exactly what he threatened. Reaching the back bleachers, Jimmy sat down and dropped me over his lap.

"Now, Theresa, tell me, do you always wear skimpy shorty shorts on the field?"

That's what this was about, my shorts? I began to laugh at the ridiculousness of the question and of the situation. Seriously, he had himself all tied up in knots over my shorts. They happened to be my most comfortable shorts. If he found them too revealing, that was his problem. "Yes, now let me up, you brute."

His hand came down on my ass, making a loud *thwack* sound. I peered around, praying no one was watching or within hearing distance. Thankfully, the few runners who had been running around the track had left. Jimmy continued to pepper my ass with his hand.

"Yes, what, Theresa?"

"Yes, I always wear these shorts when I work out. So what?"

He delivered ten more smacks, these much harder than the rest. "Yikes, ouch, stop, please, please!"

He sat me up. "If I catch you in those again, I'm going to belt your ass."

"What, why?"

"Right now, Theresa, I have four guys in the car dreaming about planting their dicks in your sexy ass. Jesus, Theresa, I don't want anyone visualizing that."

My face flushed, surely matching the color of my bottom. Jimmy cupped my face and gently pressed his lips against mine. His tongue stroked mine as one hand grabbed my hair, holding my head hostage while his tongue explored my mouth. "Mmm, you taste delicious," he hissed. His other hand reached between my thighs. The heat from the spanking created a delicious warmth in my woman parts. Jimmy's hand was stroking that into an intense inferno of need deep within my core.

Jimmy slid a finger under my shorts. "Oh, baby, I see you enjoyed your trip down memory lane."

I pulled back. "Fuck you, Jimmy." I made to stand up and leave, but Jimmy had other ideas. He pressed me onto his lap and pulled out his android. "Al, you guys head to the pub; I'll meet you there shortly." He switched off his phone and put it away in his pocket.

"Okay, little girl, you have two choices. I can pull your shorts down right here and give your ass a good thrashing. Or, we can go to your house and finish this in private."

"Or choice three, neither!" I sulked.

He chucked my chin up so our eyes were level. "Then I choose," he assured with finality.

I hated to admit it, but his words made my pussy clench. I was tempted to see what he would do if I pushed a little more. *What else would he do?* "My house."

"My house, what?"

"My house, please," I sneered.

"Wrong, princess, it's my house, please, Sir. Don't worry T, by the time I'm done, you will know how to offer respect."

Ugh, infuriating man! We stood and headed to the car, his hand an iron band around my wrist. "Give me the keys, Tesoro."

I reached into my running belt and handed him the keys. Ten minutes later, we pulled into my driveway. He got out and opened my door, pulling me out of the car and into his arms in one move. He squeezed my ass.

"Ouch," I yelped.

He grinned, capturing my bottom lip between his teeth and giving a gentle tug. Everything he did was to dominate. My mind screamed at me to tell him he had no right, but my body told a different story. I wanted this, wanted him. Isn't that why I went to the Falcone's in the first place?

It wouldn't have mattered if I changed my mind and wanted to stop this, as when Jimmy made up his mind, there was no changing it. I would keep my mouth shut and give him no reason to continue. He would finish early and leave. Then I would shower and get myself off because I was so horny, I needed the release.

He unlocked the kitchen door, the one we had used as kids, and marched us to the living room.

"Bend over," he said, pointing at the arm of the couch.

"No." I shook my head. So much for not provoking him; clearly, my sanity had taken a vacation.

"No? But your body says yes, Theresa. You're wet. I can see it even with your shorts in the way. Your chest, cara mia, is moving rapidly with your heart rate. Your nipples are hard and begging to be touched. Be a good girl and bend over the end of the couch, and I won't use the wooden spoon on your ass."

His words motivated me to lay over the end of the couch. "Shorts down," he ordered. I stood back up and wiggled my skin-tight shorts down over my hips and let them slide down to my ankles. I stepped out of them, hooked my shoe inside and flicked them into the air, hitting Jimmy in the face completely by accident. His expression had me in peals of laughter despite the vulnerability of my situation.

He gave me a predatory smile. "Very funny, Theresa. Now over the couch."

I was still laughing when his hand came down hard on my backside, taking my breath away. A dozen more, and my flaming ass was doing the jiggle. I had never been spanked, except that one time in the clubhouse by Jimmy.

"Theresa, why are you getting spanked?" he asked, punctuating each word with his hand.

"Because you're a tyrant who's pissed because his friends want to fuck me."

There was a pause. I think I shocked him. I certainly shocked myself. I never spoke that way, not to him or anyone. I don't know why I did it now, except I was so turned on. I think I was embarrassed and trying to deflect, or worse, seeing what would happen if I pushed back a little.

Jimmy must have read my mind. He slid a finger along my glistening lips. I moaned. "If more is what you want, princess, I'm happy to oblige." He pulled me up and marched me into the kitchen where he rifled through drawers until he found a wooden spoon.

"You wouldn't dare."

He grinned. "No? But you just asked me to, Theresa, didn't you?"

I pleaded the fifth by not responding. We marched back to the living room. This time, he sat down in the center of the couch. "Do you know how many beatings I took for you, growing up?"

I stood in front of him, naked from the waist down, embarrassed, my gaze on the floor.

"Look at me, T." My gaze shifted to his, and suddenly, I was looking at the old Jimmy, my BFF. I shook my head no.

"Too many to count, and do you know why?" I shook my head again. His voice and mannerism had shifted to the old quiet command that he had back when I knew him last, which seemed geared toward bringing me to a place of contriteness.

"No, Sir." I finally said the words I knew he had been waiting for.

He smiled in response, pleased with my obedience.

21

"Because, I never wanted anyone to touch you, Theresa, not even your father. The only spanking you have ever had was from me, right?"

I was shocked. My mind replayed all the times we had gotten caught doing something. I never got the blame. There were never consequences to my actions. Understanding dawned and, with it, an entirely new perspective of my childhood buddy.

"I wonder, now, if I should have allowed you to take some of the blame and some licks to go with it, as you seem completely devoid of respect.

"However," he continued, "as I said, the thought of anyone but me touching you was unthinkable. Now be a good girl and climb over my lap."

With my head down and eyes averted, I lay over Jimmy's lap.

"Let's try this again, Theresa. Why are you over my lap?"

"Because I wouldn't accept my first punishment gracefully earlier at the park, Sir, or the second one here."

"Good girl, are you ready now?"

"Yes, Sir, and, Jimmy, I'm sorry; I didn't know."

"Never you mind, sweet cheeks." With the word 'cheeks,' the first blow landed on the right side with a loud crack. I squeezed my buns together and gripped the couch with my hands. A dozen stinging blows landed on my backside in quick succession. When he stopped to rub my ass, I took in gulps of air. Unknowingly, I'd been holding my breath during the spanking and found myself gasping.

He slid a finger between my hot folds, and I mewled like a kitten in heat. I pressed up into his hand, desperate for relief. But he wasn't done with me yet.

"Count," he demanded.

At thirty, I hung over his legs blubbering and crying, completely wrung out. He set aside the spoon and rubbed my throbbing backside. I sucked in my breath at his touch, my ass so sore I thought I would scream. He added a finger to my pussy and rubbed from my clit to my anus with the overflow of juices.

He continued to rub all three spots, and my pain quickly changed to desire. I was about to beg for release, when Jimmy said, "Next time I punish you, Bella, I'll fuck you in the ass. Take that as your only warning."

"Yes, Sir." His words aroused me to new heights, the thought both terrifying and exciting. I tried pressing into his hand and gyrating into his thigh at the same time. "Be still," he said as his hand landed a sharp blow across both cheeks. I stayed still as he played with my outer lips. I tried to comply, but I was so horny, I couldn't help but buck my hips and moan pitifully.

"I see my little farfallina likes my punishment."

Farfallina? I hadn't heard that term in years. I suddenly felt a need to know what the term meant. Why did he say it now? My need to know temporarily overrode my need for sexual release. "Jimmy, you used to call me that all the time, what does it mean?"

He stopped stroking my outer lips and sat me up, looking into my eyes. "Farfallina means little butterfly, Theresa. You have always been my little butterfly, so precious."

For reasons I couldn't decipher, I became unhinged by his words. The tears welled in my eyes and leaked down like rain on a windowpane, continually beading and sliding. He pulled me in tight and held me while I cried, my steady dripping turning into a full ensemble of sobbing and messy tears.

Released from twelve years of life without him, I felt spent and so open. I felt like twelve years of indecision, grief, and loneliness was swept away in that simple act of surrender. Sure, I have accomplished a lot professionally. I am a strong woman, but I realized now that Jimmy had been my entire life. He had always been there, and then he wasn't.

I pushed him out of my life when his family moved away from our neighborhood, punishing him for leaving me. Twelve years later, here I was, coming to terms with that fact over his knee. All I'd accomplished was alienating the Falcones and making myself miserable. The petals of awareness came at me in a flurry as I bawled my eyes out on Jimmy's lap.

"Sh, Tesoro, everything is okay; you're going to be fine."

My bawling slowed down to hiccups and snuffles, the aftermath of my release leaving me feeling vulnerable.

"You left me," I accused with none of the venom I'd felt earlier.

"I know, vita mia, and I am sorry. I had no power then. I was not the master of my life like I am now." I pulled back, grabbing a few tissues from the box on the coffee table. I felt self-conscious of my nakedness. I excused myself and went to the bathroom for my robe. When I came back, the living room was empty. Jimmy was gone. I rolled my eyes. Typical Italian.

But it was just as well. I was due to meet Robert for tapas and drinks, and I had just enough time to shower and get dressed before I needed to leave.

Chapter 2

Jimmy

I had to get out of there; the guys were waiting and hearing the words, "you left me," almost broke me. It was why I never sought her out when we lost contact, not long after we moved. I didn't want the quiet hurt she'd displayed the one time we connected after the move. I couldn't handle knowing I'd let her down, abandoned her.

I arrived at the bar and downed several beers in quick succession and then headed over to the pool table to challenge Al to a game. I was leaning far over the table, reaching for my shot, thankful for my six-foot-two-inch frame. I lined up my shot, and as my pool cue slid through my fingers, something caught my peripheral vision. I scratched my shot and stood straight, swearing and looking around for my distraction.

My inner beast reared its head when it realized the distraction was Theresa. She didn't see me as her back was toward me, her mini skirt clad ass heading toward a table on the other side of the bar by the front window. A tall, slim man, fashionably trendy, stood and gave her a hug. He passed her a drink, which she seemed grateful for and downed.

"Hey, boss, isn't that—" Al began.

I held up my hand to shut him down. Theresa chose that moment to glance in our direction as she was setting her empty glass on the table. As her eyes fell on me, her pouty lips forming a perfect O. She missed the table completely, her glass smashing to the floor. All eyes turned her way.

She blushed furiously as she jumped off her stool and bent down to pick up the shards of glass. I stalked over and picked her up and placed her back on her stool. "Stay," I commanded. I quickly picked up the shards of glass and took them to the bar to be discarded and ordered her another drink. I returned and handed it to her. "Try to keep this one in your hands, amoré."

She blushed a beautiful pink. The guy she was with stood and reached out his hand to shake mine. Theresa hopped off her stool, placing herself between us. I was a little loaded, having not eaten anything and downing five pints. I could tell she was nervous that I might do something.

"Jimmy," she said cautiously, "this is Robert. Robert, this is Jimmy, and we are leaving." She made to push past me as the skinny dude hurriedly pulled bills from his wallet to leave on the table for their drinks.

"Where do you think you're going, little girl?"

She whirled around, her face angry. "Stop calling me that, Jimmy. I'm a woman, not a little girl."

I leaned into her, my body just touching hers. A small gasp escaped her gorgeous pink lips. "Yes, you are, Theresa. Very much a woman, and a very sexy one at that." I stroked her throat and her eyes fluttered; she wanted to surrender but she wouldn't, not with Robert there.

"As a woman, you must realize what a tantalizing morsel your derriere was offering up today. Really, T, bent over in those shorty shorts for anyone to ogle, but your time over my knee, turning your fine ass beet red corrected that, didn't it?"

She gasped then steeled herself, all surrender gone. Her icy blues glared at me. "What happened to you, Jimmy? I don't know if I like the adult you. I do know I miss my best friend." A tear slid down her cheek. She picked up the drink I gave her, chugged it and slammed the glass down. She grabbed Robert's hand and stalked out of the bar. My inner beast was now quelled by her tears and her words.

I found myself unwittingly sober. It was time to go home. I paid my tab and waved goodbye to the guys. I walked the half hour back to the football field and my car. I had plenty of time to replay the scene that had happened. I knew it was wrong, even while I was doing it, but that woman did all kinds of crazy to me. The beast in me wanted to devour her. I needed a new plan, one that allowed for her forgiveness.

When I arrived home, I found Maggie on her laptop chatting happily with her girlfriends. I stopped to watch her. She reminded me so much of Theresa at that age. In a few weeks, my Maggie would be turning thirteen years old; the age Theresa was when I marked her as mine.

I looked at Maggie, so young and innocent, happily so. I couldn't imagine her having a friendship like T and I did. I couldn't imagine anyone marking her the way I'd done to Theresa. But then, Maggie had a father who loved her and took care of her. Theresa had no one, only me; the epiphany struck, it was so simple.

Theresa needed her childhood Jimmy. She needed to know I was still the safest person on earth for her, that, with me, all was possible, and most importantly, that she could be herself without recrimination. Thanks to Maggie, I had the beginnings of a plan forming in my mind. I headed to bed, and while I lay waiting for sleep to claim me, I laid out my steps.

I woke before Maggie and made my way down to the kitchen. Pops had left for Florida, his parting words, 'be back at Christmas.' I think he wanted to escape everything that reminded him of Ma, including Maggie and me.

With his departure, the mansion felt like a huge void. Without my parents, the place needed some life to fill it up. Once I got Theresa talking to me again, I was going to have her help me with Maggie's thirteenth birthday party. I would claim ignorance, guilting her into helping. I knew Mags would support the idea as the two of them hit it off. But first, I needed to apologize.

After breakfast, I drove Maggie to school, and before heading to work, I stopped by Theresa's favorite coffee shop. I watched her with the staff, and after she left, I went in. I spoke with a cute little blonde with perky tits.

"What can I help you with, big guy?" She winked and licked her lips.

Inwardly, I rolled my eyes. Outwardly, I gave her a million-dollar smile. "Do you know that woman who just left?"

"Theresa? Oh, yeah, she's a regular, why?"

"I'd like to buy her morning coffee for the next month."

She grinned at me conspiratorially. "But I'd like it to be our secret…" I glanced at her nametag, "Cindy, and here is something for you to seal our deal." I handed her an extra one hundred dollars for her secrecy.

Her eyes grew big, then she winked as she slid the money into the back pocket of her skin-tight jeans. "You got it, mister," she finished and strutted away. My next project, lunch. I knew nailing the exact time would be a little more challenging as her schedule was her own. She had routines, like on Wednesdays and Saturdays, when she volunteered as a coach at LaSalle University for the track team.

Coffee every morning at the same time and meeting up with Robert for beers and food on Sundays were her only other regularly scheduled events. My earlier 'research' was proving useful. Upon further inquiry from the guys and the bartender, she rarely frequented that bar, if ever, as no one could recall seeing her there. I didn't recall ever seeing her juicy ass at the field on Sundays before and wondered if both the bar and the location for her workouts were new. And if so, how come? Or was it all simply a fluke?

I headed off to work for a few hours, and later, on my way to another site, I stopped in at John Hopkins Hospital, where Robert, Theresa's new best friend, worked. His schedule included the bar I'd seen him in with Theresa the day before, at least once per week. Being a regular, the bartender knew where he worked and even suggested that he was gay. I was hoping to confirm that.

When I arrived, I was directed to the sports medicine department of the hospital and into the physical therapy wing on the main floor. Robert was having lunch in his office and agreed to see me. He poked his head out of his office but kept his distance.

I held up my hands and said, "I just want to talk." He waved me in, and I sat down in front of a desk loaded with case files. "You're a busy man; I appreciate you taking the time." He nodded but offered nothing in return. "Look, I want to apologize. I had just finished playing ball and I downed too much beer. The beast I usually keep safely locked away decided to rear its ugly head, and you and T just happened to be there, my apologies."

Robert smiled. "I accept, but it's not me you should be apologizing to." So, the guy wanted to bust my balls.

"Yes, I am aware, thank you."

"You humiliated Theresa yesterday. I've never seen her so upset."

Good time to find out the truth about their friendship.

"Are you in the habit of seeing her upset?" An edge was creeping into my tone. Who did this little shit think he was?

He sat back and studied me or perhaps was articulating his next words. "Well, I'm her best friend and got her through her father's death."

"Second," I said quietly. "Second best friend."

He sighed, exasperated. "Look, Jimmy, I know you two have history. I've been hearing stories about the great and wonderful Jimmy for almost eleven years. Why are you here talking to me?"

I sighed, sitting back in my chair. This wasn't going as planned; the guy just needed to come out of the closet with me, so I knew he posed no threat. "I'm here to extend the olive branch and ask for your help."

That surprised him.

"But first, I need to know. Are you gay?"

He let out a bark of laughter, not expecting such a direct question, I presumed.

"You are a very direct man, aren't you, Jimmy Falcone? Yes, I'm gay and married to my best guy friend. Theresa was my best man at the wedding last year."

Hmph, never thought much about gay marriage and I found myself picturing what a gay wedding might look like. "That's cool, congratulations," I said.

"Yeah, so I will not be competing with you for Theresa if that is what you wanted to know. Theresa and I met at university at a lecture on sports therapy. We took our passion, me, turning mine into a career in sports medicine. My much smarter and wealthier friend turned hers into a blogging career."

I chewed on that for a moment. "She has always been a gifted writer. Is her blog personal?" I thought maybe the timeline answers I needed for her next surprise might lie in reading her blog.

"No, she keeps her private life very private, no social media pages, strictly professional. So, you can imagine you outing her at the bar yesterday was horrifying for her. Ever since that Steve douche in college, she has never dated or even hung out with any other men, other than myself and my husband Josh. We're safe for her, so she lets herself relax around us."

I felt myself bristle. "What Steve in college; what did he do to her?"

Robert gazed at me, assessing. "Do you really want to know, Jimmy?"

I nodded, not trusting myself to speak.

"Steve Gibson was a recipient for the track scholarship, just as Theresa was, but he was from Central. That was your school, wasn't it?"

He continued, not waiting for an answer from me. "He pursued her relentlessly. Theresa was favored by the staff. They loved her and Steve knew she was the first choice for the junior coach position upon graduation. At the time, that was her dream. Steve was a business major and well liked by the staff, but he played games. I warned Theresa about the rumors flying around about him. But she didn't listen. Honestly, Jimmy, Theresa was like a lost little girl; she did well at school, and she did well in track. But with everything else, she struggled. Anyway, one night, she walked in on Steve and her roommate fucking. She walked out, disgusted. He didn't even attempt to apologize to her and instead said he was tired of fucking a cold fish and that she was more useless than a virgin.

He spread rumors around the school that Theresa was frigid, that fucking her was like fucking a statue. He knew her well enough to know she would give up the idea of junior coach, after being so humiliated. And he slid into the position after graduation."

My blood was boiling; I was going to kill him. "What the hell! What kind of douchebag would do that?"

Robert smirked, "You mean, embarrass her publicly? Like you did yesterday, or take what they wanted from her and then leave? Uh, like you did yesterday."

I hated the little shit, but he was right, and what's worse, I had done things to women, maybe not as bad as Steve, but I had discarded many with no regard to their feelings. I'd truly fucked up. "Robert, I'm not that guy. I love Theresa and it's time for me to woo the socks off her."

"I agree, Jimmy. How can I help?"

Theresa

It had been two days since Jimmy humiliated me at the bar. I knew seeing me with Robert had set him off. He was drunk; I know that, but it still made it hard to just forgive him. Unwittingly, he had embarrassed me beyond what I would tolerate. But he didn't know about Steve, maybe if he had, Sunday wouldn't have played out like it did.

Should I forgive him was the question I'd been asking myself since the incident. His actions at the bar hurt me, but instead of feeling righteous indignation, I felt confused. What we shared before the bar, that was real. The release, letting go of the frustrations and pain from the previous twelve years had been amazing. I was inclined to chalk up his bad behavior to bad timing.

Any other day but a Sunday, I would have been home after our session with time to process the feelings and relief I felt after he spanked me. As it was, I was still processing them days later in addition to Jimmy's drunken actions that took place after. That's why I was confused. Any other man, or any other time, and this would not have been an issue. Maybe Jimmy was an asshole, and I'd missed it all these years.

I left the house with my head in the clouds and jogged down to my favorite coffee shop, hoping a cup of strong java would clear the cobwebs of confusion from my mind. Cindy was working, and she handed my coffee but refused my money.

"Your coffee has been paid for already, Theresa."

"Great, a stalker, that's all I need." I was about to ask by whom, when Cindy offered the information voluntarily. "I'm not supposed to say who, but this gorgeous six-foot-two Italian stud came in yesterday and paid for your coffee for the month and gave me a generous tip. I was supposed to keep that a secret. Sorry."

Jimmy. Everyone thought Jimmy was a stud muffin.

"But I don't think he's a stalker; he seemed to know you. And the guy is gorgeous, Theresa. Seriously, if you're not interested, pass along my phone number, would ya?"

"Yes, he knows me all right."

I said goodbye to Cindy and told her I'd keep her posted regarding Jimmy and left. I pondered my advance coffee purchases, wondering what he was up to. Two and a half hours later, my doorbell rang. Perfect timing for an interruption, I would answer the door and then go and find some lunch. I was starving. Opening the door, I was shocked to see a food delivery. "Enjoy your lunch, ma'am," the driver said, handing me the bag and disappearing off my porch.

It smelled Greek and delicious. I carried my bag to the kitchen and opened it to find at the top of the stack a container of tzatziki sauce, and on the lid, was a note.

'Thinking of you, love, Jimmy.'

It was tempting to send it back with a note that said, *fuck you.*' But as I was starving, I decided against it. I laid out the food and dove in like a starving woman. How did he know what I liked?

The only way was if he'd talked to someone who knew me well, and the only one who did was Robert. Jimmy wouldn't know where to find him, even if he wanted to.

I worked two more hours, and then the doorbell rang again. Opening the door, there was another surprise, a massive bouquet of flowers and attached was another note.

I'm sorry, Bella, for my very bad behavior on Sunday. Please, forgive me. Love, Jimmy xo

The number of flowers took up all four vases I owned. Just as I finished spreading them around my home, my phone lit up with a text.

Do you always answer your door before checking who it is first? Bad girl.

Jimmy? I typed back.

You may need a trip over my lap again, Tesoro, to remind you that I care and want you safe.

I hated to admit it, but this Jimmy Falcone apology was getting me hot. I chose bratty in return to get a sense of how playful he was feeling. *Thanks, Falcone, you're a real tease when you're not around. I won't be over your lap anytime soon.*

I sat back giggling and wondered how he would respond. A moment passed, when my front door unexpectedly opened. Jimmy stood on the threshold. "I see you chose to be bratty. I guess you really do want that spanking."

At his words, I felt a blush spread up my neck and across my cheeks. At the same time, my belly flip-flopped and my lady parts squeezed.

Jimmy shut the door and locked it. "Tsk, tsk, cara mia,

doors unlocked, you open the door without checking, you wear shorty shorts. I think my girl is looking for attention."

He stalked toward me, a predatory glint in his eye.

"Now wait just a minute," I started to protest, but Jimmy grabbed me and pulled me in for a kiss, shutting down any chance I had at a rebuttal. His tongue dove into my mouth, silencing me. One hand moved to my ass, squeezing, the other cupped my face, effectively holding me captive while his tongue invaded my mouth.

"Have you been naughty, Theresa?"

I wanted to give him a piece of my mind, but I felt liquid heat move through me with his words.

"Yes," I said huskily.

"Yes, what?"

"Yes, Sir." I hated hearing the words that came willingly from my mouth. But, I couldn't deny the effect that submitting had on me.

"What did I say bad girls get?" Jimmy crooned like he was asking me my favorite flavor of ice cream and not if I was volunteering to get my ass whipped.

"A spanking?" I asked brightly, hoping he had forgotten the other threat.

He grinned. "That's right, Bella, what else?"

He pressed his thumb against the bud of my opening. I gasped in response.

"That's right, cara, you get spanked and fucked in the ass."

Still locked in his embrace, Jimmy walked forward as I shuffled backward toward my bedroom. It was only twelve feet from the front door to my room. Jimmy's lips stayed on mine and his hand on my ass with one finger pressing against my virginal opening the entire time. He released me at the threshold of my room and sat on the end of my bed. He curled his finger at me in an invitation to come to him. I took the few steps to stand between his long, muscular thighs.

He rolled my spandex shorts down over my ass and down my legs. Everywhere his fingers touched set my skin on fire with desire. He hadn't begun yet, and already I was dripping with need.

He pulled down my G-string next, and I stepped out of both. He lifted my shirt over my head and undid my bra. My boobs were at his eye level. Grabbing my ass with both his hands, he pulled me in, his teeth getting hold of my nipple. I squeaked in surprise. He wrapped one of his legs around mine, imprisoning me. While he assaulted my nipples, one of his hands left my ass to run along the seam between my thighs.

"Oh, Jimmy, oh, that feels…so…good." My last words were lost in a moan that escaped my lips. He brought me to the brink of climax several times, not allowing me to release. I became a hot, wanton mess and the only thing I wanted was to come.

"Over my lap, piccolo, let me show you how good you can feel."

He brought his hand down to each cheek in succession then rubbed my ass. I moaned, pressing into his hand and grinding my hips. He proceeded to pepper my backside with a steady rhythm, the intensity picking up slowly, barely noticeable. The sensations I was experiencing were almost overwhelming.

He stopped and kneaded my tender flesh, while his other hand was sliding along my moist slit. I moaned again, "Please, Jimmy, I need to come." He stopped rubbing and started spanking again. "Soon, cara, soon."

He rained twenty of the hardest spanks on my steaming derriere, and while he did, he spoke in Italian. What he said, I had no idea, but his husky Italian, along with the spanking, was creating a deep ache inside that was driving me to the edge of sanity.

He stopped and rubbed, continuing to talk quietly in his native tongue, the steady stream of Italian calming my frayed nerves. He stood me up and had me get on my elbows and knees on the bed. "Part your thighs, Theresa." I did, and they began to shake as he licked and nipped at my swollen nub. I almost went out of my mind with the intensity of the feelings I was experiencing. He added a finger to my sopping entrance, and I came instantly, squeezing his finger as my muscles convulsed.

"You are so tight, cara mia, deliciously so." He ran his thumb from my sopping slit to my anus, pressing his thumb into my virgin bud.

"Jimmy," I squealed. Panicked, I tried to shy away.

"No, no, do not panic, piccolo."

I stopped squirming and allowed him to continue. He moved his mouth back to my opening, flicking and licking, working me up to the point of another climax. He pulled back for a moment.

"No, don't stop, I beg of you, please don't stop."

He pressed his thumb into my ass while his fingers plunged into sopping folds. I screamed my orgasm, which seemed to go on forever, my sex continuing to clench and spasm. I felt spent as I collapsed on the bed. Jimmy climbed up beside me and pulled me into a spoon position.

"I see you enjoyed that. Do you want more, Bella?"

I sighed in sheer contentment. Gazing into his face, I answered, "Yes, please."

He took off his pants and deposited them on the floor but not before pulling a condom from his pocket. When he stood, his cock also stood; he was large and very hard. He pulled me to the edge of the bed, bringing my knees up on top of his shoulders. He slid in torturously slow until seated to the hilt.

Jimmy felt massive inside of me. By comparison, Steve was considerably smaller.

"Oh, Jimmy, I crooned. He slid his cock in and out slowly, creating exquisite friction in my lady parts. "Jimmy, I'm going to come."

"No, not yet, Bella. You have to wait for me this time. If you don't, I will pull out and fuck that little back hole of yours."

He began pumping hard, taking me the way I'd always wanted, always imagined.

"Now," he grunted. We both released in shuddering spasms. I felt wave after wave of release ripping through my body. When our heart rates began to slow, Jimmy pulled off his condom and headed to the bathroom. He brought back a warm washcloth and cleaned me up. He went back and cleaned himself, I presumed, when I heard the water turn back on.

He came back to the bed and I curled into his side, my head resting on his chest. I must have dozed off because an unbidden thought of Maggie popped into my mind and I startled. "Jimmy, what about Maggie?" I made a move to get up, and he chuckled, pulling me back.

"Relax, Bella, she is at cheerleading practice. Al's wife, Tessa, is the coach and takes Maggie and their daughter, Emma, who is Mag's best friend. I will pick her up later, so, we have three hours and reservations."

"Reservations?"

"Yes, if you'll join me, Theresa?"

I hesitated. He had bought me coffee, sent me a delicious lunch, flowers, and brought me to multiple orgasms. I wanted to say yes, but I was still worried that drunk-bar Jimmy would embarrass me again.

"Theresa, if you're not ready, it's okay to say no. I was a total ass, a jealous ass, and I hope, in time, you can forgive me." He addressed my fears without me having to bring them up. I liked that and decided to take a chance.

"Thank you, Jimmy. I forgive you. Honestly, I'm just worried about it happening again."

He gently cupped my face. "Theresa, vita mia, I give you my word that drunk ass Jimmy, if he should ever rear his ugly head, will never embarrass you like that again. I'm not perfect, and where you're concerned, I'm possessive. It is important to me that we have boundaries and that you understand mine as well, Tesoro. Don't think to push my buttons with another man. We will play games, T, but trying to hurt me or make me jealous won't be tolerated. Do you understand?"

"I understand. I don't like those games, either, and I'll make a promise of my own. If you ever cheat on me, Jimmy Falcone, we are done, no second chances, capiche?"

He gave me a deadly grin. "Capiche, now go and get ready; you have half an hour. I'll be back."

"Half an hour. Where are you going?"

"Next door to shower and change."

I was shocked. "Next door, as in your old place?"

He nodded.

"Since when?"

"Since yesterday. You didn't think I would let another man move in next door to a hot thing like you? Now that I know you don't lock the doors or check your peephole before answering the door, I've got to keep my eye on you." He winked and exited the back door.

Chapter 3

Jimmy

"**D**ad, did you have a date?"

I'd picked Maggie up from Al and Tessa's and was driving back to the mansion when she posed the question.

"What makes you think that?"

"Well, you're happy and you smell like women's perfume."

A soft laugh escaped. "You don't miss much, do you, chica?"

"No, Daddy, I don't."

I deflected by asking her a question, "What about you, anyone at school catch your eye yet?"

"If I did like anyone, I wouldn't tell you. How uncool is that?"

I turned into the driveway and pulled into the garage, shutting off the engine. I turned to face my daughter. "Mags, I know not having a mother to tell things to has been hard, especially now with Nonna gone. I want you to know, I'm more liberal than you think. I'm here for you and I respect your feelings; you can share anything with me."

She gave me an accessing look, which reminded me a lot of Theresa at her age. "Prove it."

"Okay, Mia, and how do I do that?"

"Tell me about your date, but like, really, tell me, you know, not the details, yuck. But like how you felt and what you like about her, that kind of stuff."

I realized by her desire to understand the complex dynamics of my interactions with women, she was looking for a blueprint, the type of thing a mother would generally provide. I told her I was liberated, so it was time to share, and I hoped I could give her what she sought. "Okay, I'll tell you what. Let's go inside and make some hot chocolate, and I'll tell you all about my date with Theresa. I'll even throw in a bonus."

She clapped her hands excitedly. "What bonus?"

"I'll tell you what twelve-year-old boys are thinking about. But, you gotta fess up, too, capiche?"

"Capiche," she agreed, a broad smile lighting up her beautiful face.

"I love you, Mags."

"I love you, too, Dad."

Three hours later, I was heading off to bed with a smile plastered to my face. Being a friend and confidant for Maggie, instead of a parent, had allowed me wonderful insights into her thoughts and feelings. It felt natural to slide back into my role as young Jimmy, the guy who had won Theresa over, resulting in the best conversation with my daughter that I'd ever had.

My daughter and Theresa both needed the old Jimmy. I needed the old Jimmy. Being caught up in the business world since graduating, I could see that I had become serious. By nature, I'm a fun loving, playful guy, and it was time to channel that.

During our father-daughter confessional, I shared with Maggie that I wanted us to have a date night once a week. Her response had been very enthusiastic, and she'd already planned the first month's worth of daddy-daughter dates.

I added them to my calendar on my phone and asked her about joining Theresa and me for a night on the town. I didn't tell her the date would be a lead in to getting Theresa to help with her birthday party. I would help the idea along at some point. Knowing my daughter, she would run with it, once it was brought up.

The next morning, when I woke up after a great night's sleep, I felt vigor in my spirit and a new hunger in my body. I was switched on to life and sexual desires which all centered around Theresa in my bed. I was stiff just picturing all the things I would do to her. But not today; I had special plans to unroll. I dropped Mags off at school and went straight to work. I planned on working through lunch and leaving early.

Theresa would get an Italian lunch delivered that contained spaghetti and salad. Wednesday was a training day at the university and the only day she allowed herself carbs. She didn't know it yet, but one of her track and field heroes, Al Cantello, an old friend of my father's, would be visiting her today to give pointers to the team she was helping to coach.

She had met Cantello once when he was a guest coach and she a student. At eighty-five years old, Cantello was still coaching long distance running with the naval academy. He was known as one of the world's greatest javelin throwers of all time.

I wanted a front-row seat when T realized he was there to see her and give pointers to her team. Included with her lunch delivery was a gift, a new training outfit with longer shorts and a note that read, '*Wear this today, please. You'll know why later.*' That would give her something to think about. A part of me hoped she would wear her old shorts so I could have a reason to punish her as she had the most spankable ass.

I left work at 2:30 and drove through an early rush hour to get to La Salle University. I was still a distance away when I saw T enter the field wearing her new outfit. I pulled up and sat in my car by the field. Just as warm-ups began, I saw Al enter the training area and approach T. She was stunned, her expression of shock evident, even at this distance. She quickly shook hands with her hero and offered him a chair, which he declined. Then she looked up, looking for someone. When she spotted me in my car, she gave me a radiant smile.

Then the show began, with T joining her team and benefiting from Al's teaching along with the others. She stopped often to write notes. This was the most focused I'd ever seen her. I never knew that running and training were such a huge part of who she was. When she was thirteen, she was just getting into track, and I missed the transformation that led to the incredible athlete I saw before me.

And then I saw Steve. He wasn't supposed to be there. Robert had told me that Theresa volunteered on Wednesdays, only because it was Steve's day off. I got out of my car. If he tried anything with T, I would nail him. I walked nonchalantly over to the field and entered through the same doorway Al had gone through.

Steve was standing in front of Theresa talking to Al. I walked right over and shook Al's hand, disrupting Steve from whatever monologue he was boring the old athlete with. "Hello, Mr. Cantello, I'm Jimmy, you know my father, James Senior."

"Jimmy, I just spoke with your father yesterday. I was sorry to hear about your mother. Maria was a wonderful woman."

"Thank you, sir, she was a wonderful woman and a great mother. I guess you've met Theresa. My mother helped raise this fine athlete you see before you."

His eyes took on a new appreciation for Theresa. "She is a very talented coach. Why is it the university hasn't scooped you up, Theresa?"

My girl looked uncomfortable, especially with Steve standing there glaring at her. I turned my attention to Steve. "Both Steve and Theresa were up for the position. It's too bad, in the end, politics won, and the better coach is now a volunteer."

Al, being old school, tried hard not to laugh at me outing Steve. Theresa's cheeks heated but not out of embarrassment. She looked to Steve to see what his reaction would be, and sure enough, he'd risen to the bait. "I'll have you know, Falcone, I got the job fair and square. I deserved it." He couldn't hide the hate in his voice.

This man might be a talented competitor, but he had no love for people. "You're right, Steve, and embarrassing Theresa and lying about her conduct had nothing to do with you getting the job. You knew you couldn't get it on your own, so you contrived a way to get rid of her. Well done, poor sportsmanship, though. And not very honorable. What do you think, Al?"

You could hear a pin drop. The entire team stood still, waiting for a comeback from Steve. This was a pivotal moment as the head of the track and field was listening, the team was listening, anyone who mattered was listening.

"Who the fuck do you think you are, Falcone? What, did Theresa come whining to you about how I screwed her over all those years ago? She couldn't have handled the pressure; I did her a favor."

Before anyone else had a chance to react, Theresa faced him directly.

"You're right, Steve, the night I walked in on you having sex with my roommate, Ramona, you belittled me for the last time. I couldn't handle that type of pressure. So, if that is what you think it takes to run a team, then I guess you were the best candidate. But I am a winner, a champion, and I love this sport and these competitors."

She held her arms open to all the students there. "And I will do whatever it takes to make them the best they can be, because I care, and I can. This man," she looked at Al Cantello, "is my hero because everything he does is with integrity and hard work. He is still considered one of the best American competitors of all time. That is what I emulate whenever I step on this field, honor and respect for the sport and for my teammates. You, Steve, are nothing, and when you step on this field, I'm embarrassed. Because, deep down, you know you don't have the mindset, you don't have the passion, and you don't have compassion. Deep down, all you really care about is you."

She sneered the word you. I was shocked; that was the old Theresa. The team around her clapped. I guess Steve wasn't very popular with the athletes. The head of the team, Tom Patterson, motioned to Steve to follow him inside.

"Well, Jimmy, Theresa, this was more than I bargained for. Theresa, you are a very kinetic athlete, you are training kids six years your junior, and you're working hard to keep up, but the fact remains, you're keeping up. With extra training, there is no reason why you couldn't go back to competing if you have a desire to, or full time coaching. I, for one, would love to see you working in this field. You have fire, girl, and passion, good qualities in an athlete."

Theresa was stunned and flustered. I shook Al's hand. "Thank you for coming today, Mr. Cantello; it was a real honor to see you again, sir."

Theresa looked at me with surprise.

"You, too, Jimmy. Tell your father I'll be in Florida next week, and I'm taking him up on his deep-sea fishing invitation."

"Will do, sir."

"Theresa, I hope to see you again, young lady. Good job and keep up the great work."

With that, Mr. Cantello walked off the field, followed by the team, plying him with questions.

I turned to Theresa. "Nicely done, T. I wasn't sure you had it in you. I was prepared to be your knight in shining armor and dismount the bad guy."

She laughed. "How did you know about Steve? Did you know he would be here?"

"No, I didn't. I arranged for Al to be here as a surprise for you. I guess Steve caught wind of his presence and decided to come of his own accord. As far as how, Robert mentioned him to me and a little about what went down."

She seemed to consider my words.

Before she could ask more, I said, "How are you feeling about that interaction? I mean, you just verbally beat up a guy who degraded you and stole your job. You must feel some vindication?"

"I feel good, Jimmy, like I just took something back that was mine. Not a job, but my self-respect. I never would have done it if you hadn't been here, so thank you for that."

I nodded. She had a long way to go to restoring herself, but today had been a big step. "I'm proud of you, Theresa, you were perfect." I grinned. "Are you free to go?"

"I have another hour here."

"Okay, well, I have another surprise. I'll text you the time and location. Good job today, bella, I'm really proud of you."

Her face lit up. "Thanks again, Jimmy. I couldn't have done it without you." She stood up on her tiptoes to kiss me, and I pulled her in tight. I could feel how wound up she was. My surprise would do her good.

"Later, bella," I said and headed toward my car. I pulled out my phone and made a call to my cousin, Louisa, a premier masseuse. I set up a time for an appointment at 5:00 and then texted Theresa the address. Later that night, I received a text from Theresa.

> *(Theresa) That was an amazing gift, thank you.*
> *(Me) You're welcome, Tesoro.*
> *(Theresa)* Jimmy
> *(Me) Yah?*
> *(Theresa) Can I ask you a question?*
> *(Me)* Yah
> *(Theresa) How did you know that was exactly what I needed?*

There were many things I could have said, many of which would have stroked my own ego. But that was not what she was asking; she wanted to know how I knew her so well.

> *(Me) I'm observant when it comes to the woman I love, piccolo.*
> *(Theresa) Thank you, Jimmy. "lip emoji"*
> *(Me)* T?
> *(Theresa)* Yah?
> *(Me) Mags and I would love it if you would join us for a night on the town this Friday.*
> *(Theresa) "heart eyes emoji, thumbs up emoji, smiley face emoji, two heart emojis and a wink emoji"*

I laughed at her use of emojis and sent a reply in the form of four emojis. A crazy one, an ass one, a spanking hand and a muscle arm.

(Theresa) OMG, Jimmy! Seriously, you have an ass addiction.

(Me) Only for you, bella. C U at 3, T.

(Theresa) Okay Jimmy, thanks again. "heart emoji"

Chapter 4

Theresa

I discarded my phone and rolled over on my bed. I was so relaxed, the idea of moving to find food was out of the question. This had been the best day ever. Something inside of me that I'd locked away in my first year of college stirred. I felt sassy, instead of afraid. Alive, instead of a shell. Inspired, instead of tired and hopeful, that was the best one, hopeful that maybe my life was finally on the upswing.

On Thursday after my lunch was delivered, this time, steak and salad, both done to perfection, I decided I needed a plan. I was a recluse, and my wardrobe was limited. I phoned Jimmy to find out what would be appropriate.

"Hello, farfallina, to what do I owe the pleasure?"

"Um, I was considering what I would wear tomorrow, but as our location is a secret, I wanted to know what would be considered appropriate for our outing?" I felt stupid; I often did. I was blushing, geez, what was wrong with me? I was glad I wasn't talking to Jimmy in person, at least he couldn't see me blushing.

"For stage one, something comfortable and layered as we will be outside."

"Oh, I see, well, can I ask what we will be doing?"

I heard him laugh. "You can ask all you want, Tesoro, but you will not get an answer. Mags and I will pick you up at 3:00. Be comfortable and maybe a sweater."

"Okay, see you tomorrow." I hung up the phone.

Friday came, and I was a nervous wreck all day. I followed my usual routine, getting my 'free' morning coffee, going home, working for a few hours. Except, today, I couldn't concentrate. I would get going on an article and only to find myself drifting, images of our date night playing over in my mind. I had a bath and shaved everything, making sure I was soft and ready in case a sleepover followed this family date.

Finally, at 3:00 the doorbell rang. I opened it to have Mags throw herself into my arms. "Theresa," she gushed, "we're going to have so much fun!"

Maggie's enthusiasm was contagious. All my stress just melted away when faced with her optimism. "I am so glad you're here. I'm super stoked about our outing."

"Daddy," she said, turning to Jimmy who was just stepping out of the car. "Do we have time to see the famous treehouse?"

He was about to answer, then he hesitated, and his expression changed. He got a gleam in his eye. "All right, I will give you a five-second head start. Go!"

I took off like a shot with Maggie on my heels. We raced through my kitchen and out my back door. She passed me as she jumped over the low fencing that separated the two backyards. Maggie made it to the ladder first in a fit of giggles, and Jimmy raced after us, making the monster sounds. I moved up the ladder after her and made it to the last rung before Jimmy caught hold of my ankle. I screeched with surprise, and

Maggie helped tug me to safety, where we lay on the plank floor panting and laughing.

A moment later, Jimmy's head popped up at the opening.

"Are you coming in?" I asked.

"I don't think so. I'm not even sure you two should be in there." A crack was heard, and Jimmy's head disappeared. Maggie and I peered over the edge to see Jimmy on his ass on the grass below us.

"Daddy, are you okay?"

He waved up and lay back in the grass, closing his eyes.

"Jimmy? Jimmy?" No response. I started to panic and flew down the ladder, landing on one side, while Maggie, right behind, landed on his other. Maggie shook him. I leaned over and listened for a heartbeat. Jimmy growled loudly, startling us both. Back in the game, we tried to get up and run, but we were too slow. Jimmy grabbed us and pulled us in. Just one of Jimmy's arms was too much to fight, and I gave in, while Mags still fought on valiantly.

"You had me worried there for a second, junior."

"Junior, really? You're going to pay for that, Tesoro."

My lady parts clenched. "I'll hold you to that," I whispered in his ear. I rolled onto my back, staring up at the clouds. "I haven't done this since forever, Jimmy. How about you?"

"Feels like a hundred years, cara."

"What does?" Maggie had also rolled onto her back to see what we were doing.

"Watch the clouds, Mag; tell us what you see."

She lay back, and I wondered what sort of picture this would make. Two grownups and a teenager lying on a lawn, staring at the sky.

"Hey, I see a cheerleader," Jimmy said, pointing.

"I don't know, Dad, I see a swimmer," she responded. And for fifteen minutes, that was how our conversation went. It was so much fun; I'd forgotten how wonderful it was to lie outside and look up for a change.

After our sky gazing, we headed into the city, to Citizens Bank park, home of the Phillies. "Wow, Jimmy, these are amazing seats," I said when we sat down in the fourth row from the Phillies' dug out.

"Pops bought them years ago, T, when the business was just starting to boom. Remember where we used to sit?"

I looked around, getting my bearings. "I think up in the two hundreds, by the left fielder."

Jimmy smiled. "That's right; good memory."

Jimmy ordered us foot longs, edible cookie dough, beer and water, and an iced tea for Mags. I decided to not make a fuss about having carbs on a Friday. Somehow, I felt I might burn off the extra calories later in the evening. At least I hoped I would.

We purchased red foam Phillies' number one fan foam fingers and had fun beating Jimmy up with them when we weren't using them to cheer the team. We left the stadium and headed toward downtown and into the core of the shopping district.

"What's next, Daddy?" Maggie's enthusiasm for our evening oozed out of every pore in her body. I wondered if I'd ever been that enthralled with life?

"You'll see, bambina."

Jimmy parked in an alley and banged on a door. I was wondering what was going on, when a woman I recognized opened the door. Jimmy's cousin, Tina, beckoned us in. The three of us entered a beautiful boutique. "Wow, Tina, this is incredible, is this your store?" She gave me a hug.

"Theresa, so good to see you, Yes, its mine, about seven years now. I guess it's been a while since we saw each other. When Jimmy told me he was bringing you to the shop, I quickly unpacked my new collection. I'm sure we'll find you the perfect outfit, bellissima."

"Outfit?"

"Yay!" Maggie squealed, giving her second cousin a hug. Tina laughed. "Okay, ladies, right this way."

I was out of my comfort zone, while Maggie was in heaven. She raced to the changing room with five dresses. "We only have an hour," Jimmy stated as he headed to a changing room with an Italian suit that Tina handed him.

When he came out, I sucked in my breath. Holy hotness, he looked amazing. The suit showed off his long, muscular legs without making him look like a bodybuilder trying to look sophisticated. His dove grey shirt almost matched his eyes perfectly. He looked taller than usual, with the double-breasted jacket widening his chest even more. Oh, God, the man was stunning. He'd had amazing looks when we were kids, his hair and his complexion such an unusual mix for an Italian.

Jimmy's light blond curls and tanned skin were right out of a fantasy. Right now, he had it pulled back in what I called a man bun, his five o'clock shadow lending an air of masculinity to the entire ensemble. I stared, unable to draw my gaze away.

Jimmy must have felt my eyes on him. He looked at me in the mirror, his eyes narrowing. "You like, mia?"

I nodded, trying to close my slightly parted lips. Instead, I licked them.

Jimmy's narrowed eyes lit up in amusement. He curled his finger at me, and I awkwardly sashayed over to his side. "If it makes you this hot, cara, I will wear it every night before bed."

My eyes dilated and my sex clenched. I was in serious trouble; this man was so addicting. Maggie came out next in a rose taffeta, full-length skirt, with white ballet flats and a white blouse.

It was my turn; Jimmy took my hand. "Come, mia, let me

help you." Jimmy chose three cocktail dresses. One in dove grey, to match him, I guess, one in ruby red with sequins and one in white. After trying on all three, we chose the grey. It was form fitting but comfortable, with room to breathe. It had capped sleeves instead of full arm, which I preferred, and a plunging neckline that didn't allow for a bra, which Jimmy preferred.

Added to my outfit were black heels and black stockings, with a matching garter belt, and a black silk wrap for my shoulders. I threw on some makeup in the changing room, and when I emerged, we were ready to go. Jimmy wouldn't let me pay for my outfit, despite my insistence.

He ended the conversation by saying, "Are you going to be bad, il mio amoré? Time to devirginize your cute little back button?"

I blushed furiously. "Thank you, oh, great and powerful Jimmy, sir, for this finely made, sexy outfit and remarkable day, and what I'm sure will be an extraordinary evening."

He laughed then asked Tina to take some photos of the three of us.

Our next stop was the RL2, a restaurant I'd heard of that boasted the best views in the city. It sat on the thirty-seventh floor of 2 Liberty Place, and when the elevator doors opened, I saw first hand that the reviews hadn't exaggerated. The remnants of sunset still hung in the sky, making purple, orange, and pink streaks. Twilight offered the most beautiful blue, and enough of the city was lit up to make it look like the night sky was invading earth in a bath of twinkle lights.

We were escorted to our table, set back in a private section of the restaurant. Maggie was invited by our hostess to a private showing of the restaurant. "Wait till I tell Em," she said, happily following our hostess. Jimmy laughed and shook his head. "That girl, T, sometimes I wonder how I got so lucky."

I was about to respond that it was because he was such a

wonderful and caring father, but Jimmy spoke first. "I figure we have fifteen minutes; take off your panties and hand them to me." The change in the direction of the conversation caught me off guard.

"Here?" I squeaked?"

"Do not worry, amoré, they will leave us with our pre-dinner drinks; this is a private space. Come now, time is ticking, and obedience will be well rewarded."

I'd wanted a moment like this all evening, I was only offering a bit of resistance for propriety's sake. I'd be the one giving him the show and having him panting for a change. I stood up and slid the hem of my cocktail dress to the top of my thighs. I placed my hands to the insides of my panties and slid them down my legs, slowly.

Jimmy moistened his lips with his tongue as he watched. My inner goddess did a high five. I finally let go and allowed them to drop to the floor. I turned to scoop them up so my naked ass would be staring Jimmy in the face. Then I stood and turned back around and handed them to him.

"Here you are, sir."

He reached for me and pulled me down to his lap.

"Jesus, Theresa, you're a girl after my own heart, you know that? Feel how hard you make me."

I ran my hand over his bulge, and he began muttering in Italian. To me, he said, "You drive me insane. I need to be inside you tonight. Come and spend the night with me."

With those last words, he plunged two fingers inside me, eliciting a guttural moan on my part. He began finger fucking me, working me to a quick climax. "But, what will Maggie think?" I managed to pant through my moans.

He suddenly stood me up and slapped my ass, sending me to my chair. As I was placing my napkin on my lap and muttering about not coming, Maggie made her entrance and, on her heels, the waiter with our dinner.

During our meal, Maggie filled us in on her tour. After our plates were cleared and dessert and coffee ordered, Jimmy said, "Mags, didn't you want to ask Theresa a question?"

"Yes, thanks, Daddy, for the reminder." Turning to me, she said, "In a few weeks, it's my thirteenth birthday, and I was hoping." She paused. "With Nonna gone, I would like some help planning my party. I was hoping it would be you. Please say yes."

Why did I feel like Jimmy set this up? I looked at him for answers, but his face was set like a pro-gambler, blank. "I'm honored, Maggie, but with all those female cousins, wouldn't you rather have one of them help you?"

She pretended to pout. "Not," she said in a peal of giggles.

"Maggie," Jimmy chided.

"Please, Theresa," she added, "you are the premier blog queen, all my friends want to meet you."

"Okay, okay, you win. I would be honored, Princess Maggie. Make a list of what you want, and we'll get started."

"Well." She looked at me shyly. "I was hoping if you spend the night, maybe you could take me for breakfast. Daddy's working tomorrow, and we could hang out for a little while."

My eyes flew to Jimmy's, but his held an earnest surprise. Clearly, his daughter knew more than she let on.

"You're on, Mags," I said, using Jimmy's nickname for her.

Then we both looked at Jimmy, and he looked a little nervous. "I think I need to keep my eye on you two."

Maggie and I looked at each other. I was feeling a little rebellious. "Yep, better hide the weapons and the money. Maggie and Theresa are in town and we're dangerous."

We laughed uproariously and fist pumped each other. Jimmy slid his hand down over his face. *Ha*, I gloated, *Jimmy was in for more than he bargained for.*

56

Chapter 5

Jimmy

Those sassy girls, I would have to work hard to keep the two of them under control. Maggie fell asleep in the car on the way home. Once we were parked, I opened the car door and tried waking her up. She mumbled but didn't move. I scooped her up while T unlocked the door and followed behind me. When we arrived at her room, Theresa stood back out of the way. I removed Maggie's hair clips and shoes, all the while chattering quietly in Italian.

Next, I pulled her pajamas out of a drawer and walked her, with pajamas in hand, to the bathroom. She closed the door and a minute later re-opened it. I went in and washed her face and waited for her to brush her teeth then tucked her in, all the while very aware of Theresa's presence behind me. Maggie was back asleep by the time I joined Theresa at the bedroom door.

The sexual tension that had started at the boutique and followed us to the restaurant was replaced with something else. I felt less predatory but just as turned on. My awareness of

Theresa being here with me in a very natural, family setting was something new for me. I never shared my private life with any woman. I dated on and off, but mostly, I went out and had sex. There was never a shortage of volunteers, but not one of them ever sparked in me a desire for more.

This was different. I felt like we were a family. Of course, that was what I wanted, for Theresa and Maggie to like each other. But I'd not felt it in terms of the three of us. This was a first for me. I'd always wanted Theresa, but when I was given full custody of Maggie, I was so young, the idea of finding Theresa and wining and dining her seemed ridiculous.

My daughter was turning thirteen. I was twenty-eight, and Theresa would be twenty-seven on her next birthday. We were fast approaching the dreaded thirties when people started to settle down and have a family. I'd had Mags so young. Other than Al, who is four years older than I am, I don't have friends who have children. I chose my bed and was prepared to spend most of my life alone. But with T back, life was a do over and I felt a shift in my chest.

With this new family vibe, a taste of what could be, I was entertaining the idea of what I wanted for the rest of my life, how I wanted things to go. Today, Theresa reminded me, many times, of the girl I'd fallen in love with. But her aloofness was something new, her lack of confidence also new, and it killed me that I'd not been there to prevent it, that a few losers had messed her up, but I would help her change all that.

"Let's have a nightcap, amoré. I need to talk to you." I took her hand and we headed down to the kitchen. "Wine?"

She nodded, looking nervous. "Did I do something wrong?"

And here was my quandary; my cock loved the little submissive in her. But my heart hurt when I remembered the fierce Theresa who used to be. I wanted her submissive to me because she trusted me, trusted that I could take care of her, not because of fear. What did she fear, rejection? This was what I needed to find out. We took our glasses to the patio and sat by the pool. I played with the remote and turned on the pool lights and some music.

Frank Sinatra crooned softly from the surround sound. I held my glass and sat back in my chair studying her. She gazed down at her lap. "Theresa, look at me." Her gaze traveled up to my face and finally landed on my eyes. "Tell me what happened to you, bella."

She visibly stiffened. "I don't know what you mean." She was taking the denial route. I would have to get her confession another way. I reached out my hand and she took it. I pulled her over my lap and held her still. She protested but weakly, like she knew what was coming and accepted it.

I shimmied her dress up over her hips and got a spectacular view of her ass. She had the best ass ever. I brought my hand down hard, no warm up. I wanted a confession. I didn't want games or history or anything between us. I rained down the blows quickly, not giving her time to catch her breath.

After thirty, she gave in. "Okay, okay, stop please, I'll talk. You moved, and nothing was the same." She hung limply over my lap, talking to the ground, but I could hear her fine.

I started up the spanking again, her cheeks now a deep rose red. She squealed and gasped and begged, but I wouldn't let her up. Finally, she stopped fighting and lay with her tears splashing on the concrete below.

"Are you ready now?"

"Yes," she sobbed.

I pulled her up. I could feel the heat from her ass through my pants and hoped what I'd done was enough. If I spanked her more, she wouldn't be sitting comfortably for a few days. "Spill."

"You moved, and nothing was the same. I guess I protected me way more than I realized." She wiped her nose and finally looked me in the eyes. So much pain reflected there, and for the first time, I really questioned the wisdom of my parents dragging me out of my hood two years before graduation and away from Theresa.

"Suddenly, it was like every asshole in our school wanted a piece of me. Remember that guy, Dan, who you didn't like?"

"Yeah," I said dismissively, "loser, what about him?"

"After you moved, he started following me home. He would try to kiss me, and I would fight him off. One day, he and a few of his pals jumped me. They'd been hiding behind the bushes by the empty lot on the block before ours. They were disgusting, slobbering all over me like a bunch of dogs. I got out of there with my virginity intact, but barely."

I felt myself gritting my teeth and willed myself to relax. I was here to listen, and I needed to stay calm.

"And every day was like that, Jimmy. Every day, it was someone. Do you hear what I'm saying? Because the Falcones left, I was fair game for anyone who hated you or had a beef with you or your family. I got chased, pushed, beaten up, kissed, and often worse. They would taunt me and say, "Oh, poor little Theresa, where's big bad Jimmy?"

My heart clenched as I knew I had done this to her. For almost thirteen years, she'd been dealing with the shit I had left behind. My big ego did things all the time back then. I would have had many enemies. I never thought Theresa would be the target to get back at me. But what better way? Kids can be evil incarnate.

"Then I got to college. I made it there with my virginity intact and a little fight left in me, and my life went from bad to much, much worse."

"Are you referring to Steve?"

She nodded. "But confronting him the other day went a long way in finally healing that wound. Thank you. Anyway,

Steve reminded me of you, at least at the beginning. He was cocky and oh so sure of himself. He was attractive and a player and always seemed to be the center of attention, like you were. He was popular, with long legs. He was a good runner, and most importantly, he noticed me. You know, like really noticed me. For the first time since you'd left, I felt special and thought I might possibly get another chance at happiness."

This was proving more difficult than I'd anticipated. I already knew where this tale was going, and I didn't want to hear it. But I had to, for both of us.

"At first, when we went on dates, I had his full attention. Then, as he became late for dates or didn't show up at all, our time together became unstable. If we were out with a group of people, he'd refer to me as his slut. He'd get me to crawl and beg for attention when we were alone, then he'd laugh and walk out the door. He would manipulate me all the time and embarrass me in public every chance he got.

Later, he would apologize and be all kissy face. The last straw was when I walked in on him with my roommate. I was prepared to just walk away and never talk about it with him or anyone else. But I think he got freaked out. His bad behavior was coming to a head and influencing how he was viewed by his peers and the faculty.

To save himself, he said he walked in on me with someone else, and good riddance because having sex with me was like being with a virgin and not in a good way. He said sex with me was like having sex with a nun."

The tears had been building and dropping randomly from her beautiful eyes. But as she neared the end, they streamed down her face. I knew she found this embarrassing, but she had to get past it.

"I snapped. I felt like I was at rock bottom. After a few weeks of the rumor mill taking its toll, I did the unthinkable. I went to our old treehouse and contemplated the best way to kill myself."

I went deathly still. The thought of her not being here with me, not on planet Earth, because of some douche bag made me furious, but it also made me mad at myself.

"I cried, and not just over that, but I felt so alone, so unremarkable, so nothing. I must have passed out in the treehouse, because when the dawn's light came through the windows, I woke and sat up, rubbing the sleep from my swollen eyes. A beam of sunshine pierced the treehouse and landed on the interior wall, on the exact spot where you'd carved your name. I gazed at your name until the sun shifted and then stood up, resolved that I would get through this. That someone out there cared and loved me, and that had to be enough, at least for now. I swallowed my pride, finished school, and went into business for myself, as you know, and have been living in a kind of limbo ever since."

I was touched by her tale. There I was, out cavorting and doing whatever the hell I wanted, while she had suffered, and I hadn't had a clue at the time.

"I don't go out much. I don't have any friends beyond Robert and Josh. Coming to Maria's funeral, well, I almost didn't make it. I was so stressed out about seeing you. I didn't want you to see how broken I was, and I didn't want you to think you had to fix me, Jimmy, but more than anything, more than all my fears of what you'd see, I needed to be acknowledged by the one person I have loved my entire life."

Now the tears were leaking out of my eyes. What a remarkable woman.

She looked at me intently, the tears stopping. "Jimmy, I have to know you want me because that is what you want, not because I'm a mess, not because you feel guilty, not because you think you owe me anything, because you don't."

Before I could say anything, she finished her tale, "When I

left the treehouse that morning, I found my father dead on the living room rug."

She gazed at me, this glorious, broken but incredibly strong woman. And I fell in love all over again. She was it, and she would be mine, forever.

I was a mess of emotions. I wanted to punch someone. I wanted to beat this Steve guy to a pulp, but even more than that, I felt an over whelming urge to punch myself. I was such an asshole.

"Don't," she said, grabbing my hands."

"Don't what, T, engage in self-loathing?"

"Please, Jimmy, don't make me regret telling you every-thing. I know it sounds bad. But today has been the best day in forever, please don't take it from me."

I understood that. Her words cut through my self-loathing like a sword. I would make this the best fucking night of her life.

Chapter 6

Theresa

I could tell he was mad, murderous in fact, by what my words revealed. But my plea seemed to calm his raging beast, because he scooped me into his arms and carried me through the house and up to his room like I weighed nothing. Jimmy had always been stronger and taller than everyone else. He'd towered over his classmates in school. The lanky, muscular teenager had turned into a hulk of a man. I felt safe tucked in his arms, and I realized now how truly bereft I'd been without him in my life.

I pressed my face into his chest and felt a wave of desire to always be held in his strong arms. I wished I could climb inside his skin and never leave.

"I've got you, cara mia, it's okay now. I'll make everything better, I promise." He set me in his bedroom and undressed me. I stood naked and vulnerable. Jimmy undressed and moved to the center of the bed and motioned for me to join him.

I lay on my back and he moved between my legs, wrapping his arms around my thighs. "I'm sorry," I whispered.

"T, what are you apologizing for?"

I was struggling to formulate the cacophony of emotions into words he would understand. "I guess I'm sorry that I'm not better, that I was weak, that you're getting a broken version of me."

"Theresa Romano, I will whip your ass if you ever say that again. You are not weak or broken. I marked you as mine without thinking of the consequences. It was me they wanted to break, not you, il mio amoré. I took the hottest, most promising girl in school and made her mine. Those little fuckers were jealous. You are the strongest woman I have ever met. I'm proud of you. It's me who's the shit for doing what I did. Listen, T, if I'd stayed, you would have been pregnant and married by the end of grade twelve. I thought I was doing you a favor. I didn't want that life for you. You're smart, and I wanted you to be whatever you wanted to be, not saddled with me having babies. I had no idea what you were going through. Why didn't you say anything back in the early days when you came for a visit?"

He was propped up on his elbows, looking into my eyes.

"I couldn't, Jimmy. You left, and you weren't that guy any more. I had to deal with it on my own. Now, I have a question for you. What happened to Maggie's mother? Were you in love?"

He took his finger and ran it down my moist slit. My head dropped back as a moan escaped my lips. "Enough now, mia. No, I did not love her; she was a one-night stand. She died in a car accident while out on a date with someone else. Maggie was a baby when I received full custody." I was about to ask more when he said, "Shush, I'm going to take you to places you didn't know were possible."

Jimmy leaned himself over my opening and ran his tongue along my swollen lips.

"Oh, yes," I crooned.

Jimmy's tongue dove into my pussy, driving me wild. He reached under me, grabbing a cheek in each hand and squeezing and kneading, pulling me closer to his mouth, delving deeper inside. Then he licked from my slit to my back entrance, while I bucked my hips. I wanted him inside of me badly. He held me tighter. My hands grabbed the quilt on either side of me. "Jimmy," I begged, "please fuck me."

He balanced my ass in one hand and, with his other hand, finger fucked me. I screamed my release as he continued to hammer my pussy with his fingers. Without giving me a moment to recover, he took one of his fingers and slid it into my ass. Releasing his hold, he used the other to finger fuck me, his long fingers hitting my G-spot and the finger in my ass slamming into me from behind. I was engaged in multiple orgasms, barely registering when one finished and the next began.

Jimmy stopped and climbed on top of me. He pushed in slowly, rubbing my sensitive walls. In three thrusts, I was orgasming again. Jimmy picked up speed now, and my body convulsed, a long keen filling the room. His super thrusts were coming hard and fast. My body couldn't take much more, yet I felt myself climbing to another release.

"Theresa," Jimmy panted, "when I say now, we're going to orgasm together. Ready?"

"Yes, Jimmy."

Without losing pace, he pushed my knees up to my ears, giving a different angle and different sensation. "Oh my God, Jimmy, I can't, I can't wait, I—"

"*Now,* Theresa."

We both released with a cry of passion. I could feel his hot cum through the condom.

He pulled out, and I was barely conscious when he said, "Sleep now, farfallina; tomorrow, we can discuss our plan."

I was so exhausted, it barely registered when I felt him wiping me and tucking me under the sheets.

Jimmy

Theresa was asleep in seconds; multiple orgasms and spankings can do that to a person. If I hadn't been one hundred percent resolved to make her mine before, I certainly was now. I stared up at the ceiling, thinking about Steve. Of course, I'd recognized the cocky SOB when he'd strutted out onto the field. Robert had said the guy had gone to Central with me, but as he was Theresa's age, I couldn't place him until I saw him in person. Steve Gibson, the LaSalle track and field scholarship recipient.

I had planned on avenging Theresa, but social media beat me to it. I guess one of the students had recorded the interlude with us on the field. The video was called job theft and was trending. As expected, the world of blogging recognized Theresa Romano's name, as she was considered one of the few highly successful bloggers on sports medicine and training.

Her popularity on social media was pushing for Steve to be fired from his job. He was being labeled as a sexist. I couldn't have done any better, so I was thrilled when Theresa told us at dinner that Steve was given his termination papers. She had been offered his job and was considering it. She had a week to make up her mind, and I was hoping to persuade her into accepting.

I woke early and quickly wrote her a note, which I left on the nightstand, asking her to stay for a home cooked Italian dinner.

Theresa

I woke to an empty bed that reeked of sex. I pulled the bedding off and went in search of the laundry, which I found at the end of the hall. I went back to the room to shower and dress, throwing on my fun clothes from yesterday, which had been meticulously folded and set on the padded bench in his dressing room. I looked and found my dress hung up and my shoes placed neatly beneath it. My Jimmy was a wonderful blend of the brutish dominant and thoughtful lover.

My next search took me to the kitchen for coffee. I found an espresso machine and ground some beans and, a minute later, sighed in pleasure as I took my first sip. I texted Jimmy.

> *(Me) What if I say no?*
> *(Jimmy) Then I'd tell you only bad girls say no and get over my lap.*
> *(Me) "Two smiley emojis and a crying, laughy emoji" yes*
> *(Jimmy) Good girl. Picking up groceries on the way home, see you at 5.*
> *(Me) I can shop for you if you give me a list.*
> *(Jimmy) No, bella, then you'd know my secret ingredients; that won't do.*
> *(Me) I wish I'd paid better attention when your mom was teaching us to cook. I kinda suck, sorry.*
> *(Jimmy) That's 10.*
> *(Me) Huh?*
> *(Jimmy) 10 with my belt for saying you suck and apologizing for it! "Mad emoji"*
> *(Me) Oh. Um. Okay. See you later.*

(Jimmy) Sir
(Me)?
(Jimmy) Come on, mia; say see you later, sir.
(Me) Sir "kissy emoji and angel emoji"
(Jimmy) "peach emoji and hand emoji"

I laughed, setting my phone down as Maggie walked in. "Good morning," I said.

"Ugh, need coffee."

I didn't question her request, just made her an espresso. She sat and sighed in contentment when I handed it to her. I giggled.

"What?" she asked.

"Oh, nothing, well, you remind me of me, actually."

She grinned.

"Your father is making us dinner. He said he'd be home at five. Are you okay getting stuck with me for the day?"

"Oh, yeah, I am. What are we doing after breakfast?"

"I was thinking we'd go to my place and do some planning, and I'd love to get a change of clothes. Oh, I don't have a car."

"Yes, you do."

"I do?"

"Yeah, we have like seven in the garage; take your pick."

"Seven, wow, okay. Um, are you sure your dad won't mind?"

She shook her head.

"Okay, so, your birthday, what's our budget for this party?"

"Budget? Good question. I'll ask tonight."

"How about numbers, any idea how many people you'd like to invite?"

"Um, I don't know, Theresa. What did you do for your thirteenth birthday?"

"Honestly, not much. Jimmy's mom baked a cake and made me a special dinner. My dad was working, and I didn't have any close friends other than Jimmy. After dinner, he and I went to the arcade and played video games for hours. It was fun."

She sighed dreamily. "What was my dad like at fifteen?"

"Tall, confidant, like now, and super cute."

She laughed. "Come on, Theresa, tell me what he was like."

"How about we go for breakfast, and I'll tell you anything you want to know about young Jimmy. Did you know he got into trouble all the time?"

"I knew it! He acts all holy, and I'm like, sure, Dad."

I laughed at her imitation of the two of them. "Okay, go and get dressed."

Maggie left, and I breathed a sigh. What was I getting myself into? Not only did I know nothing about kids, but I'd never planned a party in my life. What could I possibly offer the Falcone princess? When she came back, we headed for the second garage, adjacent to the one we'd used last night. I was shocked when she opened the door. She'd said seven cars; she'd never said what kind. "Uh, Maggie, are you sure your dad is okay with me driving one of these?"

"Of course," she answered.

I was hesitant about what to choose, and then finally decided on what I felt was the least showy of the seven and took the Range Rover. Fifteen minutes later, we were laughing as I told her story after story about her dad and myself as kids.

"Theresa, did you like him?"

"Yes, he was my best friend, of course, I liked him." She was after something; I couldn't put my finger on.

"I mean, like him, like him, you know what I mean?"

"Who do you like, Maggie?" She opened her Instagram and showed me some cute guy's profile picture, who supposedly attended my old school in the hood. I looked at the profile, scrolling down. I could tell it was fake. "Do you know him?" I asked casually.

"Just from talking online. He asked me to meet him later today, but I haven't answered him yet. I want to invite him to my birthday party, though. What do you think my dad would say?"

A plan was forming in my mind at rapid speed, a way I could get her to see this guy was fake without me looking like an overbearing adult, and maybe catch a shithead pedophile in the process. "Tell you what, message him and invite him to meet up with you at the athletic park at the soccer field in an hour. If he's a nice guy, I'll make sure he gets an invite."

She excitedly started texting and received an immediate reply.

"Great, so listen, Maggie, this guy, this profile, it isn't real; it's a fake profile."

"What?"

"I make my living on the internet, trust me when I say I know a fake profile when I see it. If he'd answered that he couldn't meet, then this person could be harmless. But the fact he wants to meet you means he wants something."

She looked like she didn't believe a word I was saying.

"Look, don't take my word for it. He may not even show up. You know that pedophiles troll the internet looking for victims? Looking for young beautiful girls and boys, like you, Mags, you're the perfect fit. I don't want to see you get hurt by a cyber creep."

She sat back and accessed me like her dad. I felt my face flush. "I don't believe you, but let's say I did, what happens if this guy shows up and he's not who he says he is, then what?"

"Here's what I'm thinking. Let me dress in your clothing; we're almost the same height. I should be able to fit into something of yours. If your perfect boy shows, then you can get out of the car and tell him it was a good-natured prank, nothing more. But if anyone other than that boy comes, then you stay in the car, doors locked, and let me handle it, okay?"

She finally agreed, and we left the restaurant and headed back to the mansion.

Chapter 7

Jimmy

I hadn't been completely honest with the girls. I did have to spend a few hours at a new job site with the safety inspector, but other than that, there was nothing pressing that couldn't have waited until Monday. My main motivation was to go and have coffee with Robert, to extend a dinner invite to him and Josh for tonight. I texted Robert after I'd wrapped up with the safety inspector and caught up on a little paperwork and asked if I could pop by.

He texted back their address, so I headed over to their trendy neighborhood in Washington Park West. I arrived at a three-story brownstone and was buzzed in. I climbed the single flight of stairs to their apartment and Robert opened the door, beckoning me in.

I'm not typically a décor guy, but their apartment was stunning. I expected cold, modern furniture which seemed stereo typical of what I knew about gay décor. This apartment was filled with texture and color, and everything spoke expensive, boho chic, which was totally in. Being here, I could see some of Robert's influence in Theresa's house.

"Wow, this is some place you have."

"Thanks. Call me Bobby. This is more my style than Josh's, well, truth be told, Josh doesn't have style. He's almost militant in his desire for bare essentials living. I prefer bold colors and textures."

I sat down on a bar stool in their 70s retro kitchen, while he made us coffee. "Espresso, mochaccino, latte, what's your poison?"

"Straight up coffee, black."

I heard Bobby mumbling about tough guys and black coffee. I grinned in amusement. He was such a wonderfully harmless sort of person. I could see why Theresa liked him so much. Stylish, smart, amusing, many great attributes, and I found myself relaxing in his presence in a way I usually didn't with guys.

We moved to the living room when our coffee was ready. I really liked what he'd done with the exposed brick. "Did the apartment come with the exposed brick or did you add that in?"

"When Josh and I were apartment hunting, I had exposed brick down as a must have. And, of course, one must have duct work exposed to lend to the feel of industrial, but I don't like the coldness of the look when it's decorated with only basics, hence the bohemian décor. Josh wanted to buy every apartment we walked into, just to get the process over with."

He laughed and went on, "But I said no way, our apartment is here somewhere. Three months and thirty apartments later, I found this gem. Josh didn't even look at it. He said, if it fit my qualifications to buy it. So, yes, the brick was already exposed. Thankfully, because faux brick is so not what I wanted."

"You have quite an eye. Have you ever thought of doing it professionally?"

He took a sip of his espresso. "Yes, when I get sick of diagnosing hips and knees. Honestly, I am tired of the hospital politics. Why, are you looking for a premier designer?" He batted his eyes, and I couldn't help but laugh at his overt response.

"Yes, this is a very in look right now. Would you be interested in decorating a few apartments for display purposes, if you have the time?"

He sat up straighter. "Really? Why, I'd love to. Now stop chatting me up and tell me why you wanted to meet, other than wanting to spend time with me, of course." He winked.

I laughed again. "Originally, to confirm Steve's identity so I could exact some revenge, but I'm sure you follow Twitter and have seen the video?"

He responded with a huge grin. "I certainly have, and Theresa texted this morning to say he got his walking papers. With his lack of popularity, I can't see any universities taking him on. She was spectacular, wasn't she?"

He took a sip of his coffee. Then he added, "You're fixing all the wrongs in her life; good for you."

"That is my intention," I answered and took a sip of my coffee. "But I think she nailed that one on her own."

He nodded. "But she couldn't have done it without you, I think, and for that, I'm grateful, Jimmy Falcone."

I accepted the compliment and stood to leave. "Oh, I wanted to invite you and Josh over for an authentic Italian dinner tonight. Can you guys make it?"

"A look at the mansion I've been hearing about! Of course, we'd love to."

"It's a surprise for T."

"Speaking of," Bobby said, picking up his phone. "She's

asking if Josh is at work. That's odd. I wonder what she's up to."

I pulled out my phone, nothing. "It can't be good."

He looked up, puzzled. "How do you know?"

"Because she hasn't texted me. So whatever she is up to, she doesn't want me to know."

Robert's phone beeped. "Oh dear, not good at all."

"What is it?"

"She said she's going after a pedophile. Could this have something to do with your daughter?"

"Shit! What the? Robert, find out from Josh where they're going and text me the location, please."

I texted T from my car. No response. Then my phone beeped with a text from Bobby, telling me the athletic park soccer field.

I was across town. It would take half an hour to get to her. I hoped that whatever crazy trouble she'd gotten herself into, Josh would ensure her safety. I used my Bluetooth to call Maggie. No response. Damn those two. I swore in Italian as I pressed on the gas pedal, tailgating the driver in front of me. Damn, where had all this traffic come from on a Saturday?

Theresa

I prayed I was doing the right thing. Jimmy would lose it if anything happened to Maggie. I had texted Robert and connected with Josh.

"Theresa, what's going on?" Josh asked.

I explained, and he promised to do an IP search and meet us at the park. Now, for the tough part: looking like Maggie. She dressed me in a mini skirt, over the knee socks, white sneakers, a glitter top and a sparkly baseball cap. We were almost the same height, but my feet were bigger, so the shoes were killer. I put on no makeup, except bright pink lip-gloss, and chewed on bubble gum. Taking stock in the mirror, I thought, *from a distance, this might work.*

We arrived at the field ahead of time. I parked by the bleachers but not so close that he would see Maggie in the car. It was important for her to see him, not the other way around. I strutted over to the bleachers with my phone, looking busy and channeling my inner tween.

Being a blogger, I was very aware of tweens use of language. I glanced at the conversation this guy 'David' had with Maggie. There were so many signs that this guy wasn't real. I didn't have time to point these out to Maggie, but I would later and show her and Em the folly of following fake profiles. Assuming Jimmy didn't lose it and decide to never let me near his daughter again.

I saw I'd missed several texts from Jimmy. How did he know? I opened them up. I flinched when I read the first one, *where the fuck are you?* Followed by, *I just got off the phone with Robert.* I quickly exited my messages. I couldn't call him yet. He would interfere, and I was too committed to be stopped now.

I saw a man walking across the field from the street side of the park. My hair stood on end. It was him; I was sure of it. I texted Jimmy that I was safe and would fill him in later. I stood up and paced back and forth in my 'notice me girl walk' that I'd seen Maggie do. I pretended to be talking on my phone to a girlfriend. I stopped walking and stood with my toes slightly turned in. I felt like I was giving an Oscar winning performance.

I glanced to the bleachers only a few feet away. Josh was looking like a professional athlete doing jumps and squats. As the man got closer and I could see his face, I felt myself freeze. It was him, the same stalker from when I was fourteen. He was still going after young girls. It was all I could do not to throw up.

Shit, he might recognize me! I pulled my hat down lower over my face. Thank God I was wearing sunglasses. Back then he'd been in his thirties, and now looking a little heavier and in his forties, but I was sure it was the same guy. I waited for him to speak to me, still acting unaware of his presence as I was there to meet a kid, not a man.

"Maggie?"

"Like, whose asking?" I said, whirling around.

"I'm David's dad; he asked me to pick you up."

My peripheral showed me that Josh had moved closer and was now stretching on the grass just a few feet away, within earshot, for sure.

"Please, as if. Where is he?"

"Over in my car. Come on; I'll show you." The guy was looking around nervously. He couldn't make a move on me with Josh so close; he needed to separate me. I needed to play along if we were going to catch him in the act.

"Fine, then, but this is not what he said. He like said that I should meet him here." I started walking across the field, my phone beeping like crazy. I knew it was Jimmy, and by now, he would know where I was. I hoped he didn't show up before we nabbed this guy.

We were almost halfway across now, and Josh was doing laps around us, staying far enough away to look legitimate. The guy beside me made his move, and he moved a lot quicker than I thought he could. He pulled something from his pocket and was trying to get it over my nose and mouth— chloroform. I felt bile rise in my throat. My hat and glasses came off in the struggle.

"You're not Maggie; you're that little bitch from years ago, Theresa."

"That's right, asshole." I pulled out my mace and sprayed

him in the eyes. Josh was there in seconds, and he'd gotten the entire episode on video. He brought the guy down onto his stomach and slapped cuffs on him.

Josh hauled him to his feet, and as he did, pictures fell out of the guy's pocket. Most were of Maggie, some of other girls, and he'd written or drawn the most disgusting things on the photos. I felt ill and was relieved when I heard sirens. Josh's back up was almost here.

I looked back toward the parking lot and saw that Maggie was out of the car and running in my direction. I held up my hand and shook my head and pointed to the car. She looked and saw her dad squealing into the parking lot. She went back and I saw him wrap his arms around her, but he was looking at me. I held up my hand, with a thumbs-up.

It was at that precise moment the stalker chose to speak. "You got away from me years ago, Theresa. Too bad, I really wanted to add you to my collection. Then he laughed, and it was ugly, so ugly. I turned my eyes toward the parking lot. Jimmy had Maggie situated back in the car and was running toward us.

He slowed down when he passed Josh, who nodded at Jimmy but kept his gun pointed at the stalker.

I threw myself into his arms.

"Theresa, I'll get your official statement later. You guys need to go."

Other cop cars were now driving over the grass to get to Josh and the stalker. Jimmy let me go, and wrapping his arm around my shoulders, he marched us back across the field toward the cars.

When we got there, Maggie jumped out of the car. "Theresa," she said and threw herself into my arms. "You were incredible, thank you. I was so wrong. I didn't know." Then her eyes filled up with tears.

"I know, sweetheart, it's okay now. That awful man is

going to get what's coming to him, I promise. And look, you're safe now, bella, you're okay."

Jimmy had been watching our interaction. He stepped in now and wrapped his strong arms around us both and held us. I felt Maggie sigh and relax, feeling the power of his arms. I relaxed, too, and prayed that Jimmy would not hate me for what I'd done.

"Okay, you two have some explaining to do. Let's go home."

"Home?" Maybe he didn't hate me after all.

"Theresa, I'm taking Maggie; we'll meet you at the house." I nodded and got in the Range Rover. When I arrived, they had already parked and gone in the house. I parked the Rover and hung up the keys and stepped through the door into the house. I didn't want to face him. I wanted to run away and hide.

I heard laughter in the direction of the kitchen and headed toward it. At the threshold, I stopped and watched a very domestic scene in progress. Maggie was sitting on the counter talking to Jimmy, while he was pulling out pots and pans. They acted like nothing was wrong.

"T, come join us."

I didn't know what to expect, but this wasn't it. "Um, uh, hey, I should probably go and let you two talk about, ah, I don't know. I just, well. I just feel. Um, sorry, I'm sorry, Jimmy." I turned to flee. I had to get out before he unleashed all his fury at me.

"Stop. Theresa!"

Jimmy spoke rapidly in Italian to Maggie, something about vegetables. Then he threw me over his shoulder and marched me up the staircase and down the hall to his suite. He delivered me to the bed. "T, you've got to change your clothes. Seeing you dressed as a twelve-year-old is making me horny, which is so wrong, but first, tell me what this is about."

I didn't know what to say. Why wasn't he mad? Why wasn't he chewing me out? I knew what this was; he would fulfill the dinner obligation and then dump my ass. I couldn't take the rejection.

"I just think I should go." I made to leave, and Jimmy grabbed me and sat on the bed with me over his lap, all in one smooth move. "Maybe after I give you those ten I promised, your tongue might work." He slid the skirt up. "Jesus, Theresa, you're not even wearing underwear, and this thing barely covers anything."

He slammed his hand down on my ass. "Ouch, Jimmy, I, ouch!" He stood up after ten and told me to lean over the end of the bed. The next ten were with his belt. The first stroke landed, and I felt the bite of the leather on my skin and let out a little screech. After ten, my ass was sizzling, and the tears were pouring down my cheeks. It wasn't excruciating; it was me finally releasing my emotions from the day's events.

Jimmy sat me up and rubbed my back. "Shh, bella, it's okay now. But you had me scared today. Why did you do it?"

I was relieved he was asking and not accusing. "It started with Maggie asking me what I did for my thirteenth birthday. Then she asked me what you were like when you were a teenager. I shared lots of stories with her, but I could tell she wasn't asking me what she wanted to ask. So, I asked her who she liked, and she got on her Instagram account and showed me a picture of a kid named David. But, Jimmy, it was a fake profile. I make my money in the cyber world, so I know fake accounts when I see them. Maggie thought she really liked this guy and wanted to invite him to her birthday. He had already tried to get her to meet with him, and I was scared she would without your knowledge. You didn't know about him, did you?"

Jimmy shook his head.

"That's what I thought. Anyway, I told her to set up a

meeting because she didn't believe me about the profile being fake. I was scared for her. So, I disguised myself as her and had Josh meet me there. We had to catch the guy doing more than showing up pretending to be the father of the guy online. So, when we were crossing the field, he made his move and tried to put a chloroform-soaked rag over my nose and mouth. I fought him off and sprayed mace in his eyes. Then Josh had him on the ground, and the rest you know. I made sure she was safe in the car, Jimmy, I never would have let her near any of it. At the end, she got out of the car. She wasn't supposed to, but you came squealing into the parking lot and diverted her, thank goodness. What you didn't see were the photos that fell out of his jacket when Josh was wrestling him back to his feet. Photos of Maggie he'd downloaded from the internet, but he altered them with writing and drawing on them; they were disgusting. I'm hoping Josh has raided his house by now and taken his computer. This is not the guy's first time. I'm sorry, Jimmy, so sorry. I should have asked or told you first, I just went ahead and put your only child in danger."

"Ten."

"Pardon?"

"I told you, stop apologizing, T. Now bend over." He rained ten sizzling blows to my already sore backside. He sat me up and drew me back onto his lap.

"Jimmy, why aren't you angry? I don't understand."

"You are a hero, piccolo. As far as I'm concerned, you saved my daughter from herself and a pedophile. Who knows what could have happened had she met with the guy on her own? I have you to thank, cara, as I had no idea about this friendship my daughter was encouraging. She did not share the whole story, and now that I know, restrictions will be put in place, and later, she and I will discuss a fitting punishment. And you and I will discuss your punishment, Tesoro, not for what you did, but for not answering my messages. I was terrified for you both, and I never want to feel that again. But for now, you are the hero, and I'm grateful to you. Now get yourself cleaned up. Bobby and Josh will be here soon for dinner."

"Bobby and Josh? Oh, um, I don't have any clothes to put on, Jimmy. I should go."

"I grabbed some things for you. But first, you get ten more."

"What, why?" I whined.

"Because you're still talking about leaving, and it's unacceptable. Now bend over and grab your ankles."

I did as he asked and heard the belt swooshing through the air before it landed. A searing pain lit up my backside. This position exposed my sit spot, and that was what Jimmy was aiming for. Nine more, and I stood on trembling legs. Jimmy dropped the belt and gave me a hug.

"Come, bella, shower time."

He walked me to the bathroom. "Are you okay?"

I nodded.

"Good, the groceries I need are probably here now, so I must go and create my masterpiece. You have forty-five minutes, and when you come down, I want a smile on that beautiful face."

"Yes, Sir." I saluted.

Jimmy winked and was gone.

Chapter 8

Theresa

I was stunned at his lack of anger. He didn't yell. He didn't dump me. I was feeling deliriously happy, and five minutes into my shower, what he'd said finally sunk home. I was a hero. I was playing that word 'hero' on repeat in my thoughts.

I never thought I would hear that word synonymous with Theresa Romano. The events of earlier and the role I'd played was taking on a dreamy quality and being replaced with skepticism. Despite what Jimmy said, I felt unsure as to the wisdom of today. Of course, I still hadn't told him that I recognized the stalker. I didn't want to. All it would do, in my eyes, was cement my stupidity.

I exited the shower and stared at myself in the bathroom mirror. I didn't see a hero. I saw a young, scared woman. A woman who questioned her self-worth, who doubted herself, and as a result, had shied away from the limelight. But with the Al Cantello video going viral, and now this in the same week, news of the arrest was bound to get out, and then I would once again be in the spotlight.

I was at a crossroads with that and with regards to my burgeoning relationship with Jimmy. I felt safe and loved in his arms. I felt like an exotic flower in his bed. He brought out things in me I didn't know were there. I wanted to fuck him every time I looked at him. He incited desire, passion, and, yes, even respect for the type of man he'd become. But...he wasn't the problem. Already I was changing, my situation changing and, so rapidly, that I felt unhinged. Maybe Jimmy was more than I could handle.

Jimmy

I had Tina deliver an essential wardrobe to my place for Theresa. My only request had been that everything she chose be ultra-soft, comfortable, yet sexy. I was pleased when Theresa came downstairs right on time dressed in black silk lounging pants, with matching ballet flats and topped off with a dove grey silk camisole. Her hair was up in a loose bun held together with iridescent chopsticks that beautifully showcased her auburn tresses. She had a dusting of powder on her cheeks that held a sparkly sheen and pale pink lipstick. Her eyes looked dewy and luminescent. She was delicious, and I couldn't wait to take it all off her later.

As T entered the gourmet kitchen, her face lit up when she saw our friends. She grabbed what she needed to set the table, and the girls followed her to the dining room like little ducklings.

"Looks like she has a fan club," Josh said with a grin.

"Look out, world," elaborated Bobby. "Here comes the new and improved Theresa."

I laughed, but in the back of my mind, I wondered how she was handling the recent events. She'd gone from hiding these past six years, to suddenly being in the limelight. I knew that was not something she was comfortable with. Tessa, Al's wife, excused herself and, moments later, we heard giggling coming from the dining room.

Theresa

"No social media, Mags," Jimmy yelled from the kitchen.

Eye roll. "Yes, Daddy." Giggles from her and Emma.

"I meant it."

Another eye roll. "Seriously, Dad, I'm not on social media."

Maggie excitedly repeated the story of today to Tessa and Emma.

"Theresa, could you show me all the fake stuff to watch out for?" Tessa requested.

I agreed and had Tessa open her Facebook account on her phone, as she wasn't on Twitter, Instagram, or Snapchat. The idea was the same; it was learning to recognize the signs. By the time the gentlemen were bringing in the food, all three were prolific at detecting fake and stolen profiles.

"You know, Theresa," Al said, "You should be teaching that in schools."

Josh chimed in, "It would be very useful for parents and kids to be better equipped at reading the signs, for sure. We have a program, but to be honest, it is such a militant approach that I don't think the kids even hear the spiel. I could set something up with community policing and neighborhood watch groups if you like?"

I felt myself blanch. Oh God, more pressure. I wanted to run and hide under the blankets in Jimmy's bed.

"Well, it has been a crazy day, hasn't it, Jimmy?" Bobby said.

Jimmy's eyes were on me, intently watching my reaction. "It has indeed. I think our girl needs some time to process before she decides anything. Tonight is for celebrating."

Bobby grinned his agreement, and Jimmy picked up his wine glass. "To Theresa, the bravest woman I know."

We clinked our glasses, and the conversation veered off into many directions after that. I was relieved to get the focus off me and delighted to see the conversation take shape as our guests got to know each other better. Jimmy's best friend with his wife, and my best friend with his husband. It was fitting and turned out to be an entertaining evening.

Two hours later, Al and Tessa were taking their leave and asked if Maggie could join them. I was sure Jimmy would say no. But after Al guaranteed no social media for the girls, Jimmy finally gave his permission. With the four gone, that left us with Bobby and Josh and a statement that still needed to be given. Jimmy left us to go and make special dessert coffees and Bobby offered to help, leaving Josh and me alone.

"Theresa, Brent Oberon, the internet stalker from today, you knew him?"

I gulped; this was what I was afraid of.

"Yes, well, I recognized him from the internet. Um, okay, that's not right. I recognized him, when I saw him in person, as someone I had met about eleven years ago through the internet. He was older and heavier but the same guy."

Josh gave me an appraising look. "So, you mean you spoke with this man on the internet and then met him in person?"

"Yes."

He waited. I knew he wanted to ask me if I had been

raped. I hadn't, but the fact he was even thinking it proved to be my worst nightmare. That if this information got out, people would assume the worst. I didn't want people to think about me at all. I wanted anonymity; I was a blogger, a sharer of information, not a hero, or someone that took down pedophiles. I just wanted to share what I knew from a safe distance. If life had taught me anything, it was that people could be cruel.

I sighed, feeling suddenly exhausted. "Nothing happened to me, Josh, if that is what you're wondering. I didn't meet him. I set up a time to meet him, but I hid until he arrived to make sure. That man, Brent? He showed up in a van, just like today. Not the same one, though. Did you go to his home?"

"Yes, and that is all I'm going to say for now. Jimmy has given me Maggie's laptop, so I will be reading back through the history. For now, there is nothing else I need from you."

I wanted to ask if the guy we'd caught was as bad as I suspected he was. But Bobby and Jimmy arrived with the special coffees. Josh put away his notepad and pen, effectively ending our business, then he and Jimmy got into a discussion about how Josh and Bobby had met. Bobby scooted closer to me, and we talked about how today's events went down.

"You know, Bobby, I saw that bastard and almost upchucked breakfast. He's so lucky all I had was a can of mace."

He laughed. Then his face sobered. I guess it was like a nasty trigger. "How are you feeling about that? You must feel empowered that you were there to make sure nothing happened to Maggie. Especially after what could have happened to you."

You could hear a pin drop. Jimmy and Josh had fallen silent. "You mean Steve," Jimmy asked.

"No," Bobby said, "I mean that asshole in—" Bobby stopped, responding to my eyes going as big as saucers. "Yeah, Steve," he finished awkwardly.

Jimmy didn't buy it for a minute, but he was a gracious host. He and Josh picked up where they'd left off.

"Sorry," Bobby whispered.

"It's okay," I whispered back. "I was going to tell him eventually."

Josh stood up. "Time to go. My shift starts at 6:00 am." We walked the couple to the door and said goodnight. When the door closed, I summoned my courage and faced Jimmy. "Maybe I should get going and let you have some down time." I made to grab my purse.

"Ten."

"Excuse me?"

"Didn't I already say you weren't leaving?"

"Yes, Jimmy." I put my purse back down, relieved that he wasn't ready to get rid of me. Before I could fall into despair about feeling like a feeble-minded woman, he said, "I'll give you a head start. Go!"

I took off like a shot, but he caught up to me on the landing. I squealed as he hauled me up and over his shoulder. As I dangled down, I smacked his ass.

"You cheeky little thing," he said with a laugh.

Jimmy

I wanted to beat her ass until she screamed for mercy. She'd ignored my texts earlier, forcing me to find her through Bobby. When I came screeching into the parking lot, Maggie was just running onto the field and Theresa was waving her back and pointing to me. It wasn't until I saw Josh, holding a suspect at gunpoint, that relief flooded me like a drug. For that alone, she had it coming, but then I found out there was still more she hasn't shared. How many protective layers did she have? I was hoping I would slice through the rest tonight, so we could begin our life together without any baggage holding us back.

As I carried a squealing Theresa up the stairs, I silently thanked Josh for being there. If he hadn't been, I probably would have killed the guy. Beyond that, the most upsetting part of today for me was the loss of control. I'd been fighting my instincts since the park. Theresa was right, if I'd shared my initial reaction with her, it would not have ended well. But by holding back, I was able to look at the scenario in a different light.

She had been driven by the need to protect. I knew that feeling. I also knew the last thing she needed was to be scolded by me instead of being accepted and seen in a hero's light. Celebrating with our friends had needed to happen. But now, in private, I could share my displeasure at her reckless actions.

I loved what she'd done for Mags, but not at such a high risk. She hadn't consulted me first, and I knew why. I would have said no way, and she didn't want to be stopped. She knew there were other ways to handle the situation, but she didn't choose them. I'd been confused earlier as to why. But something had happened to her before. I picked up on it at the field, the pedophile was laughing at something when I reached T. I wondered, after what Bobby said, if she had known the guy.

I deposited her on the bed. "Okay, Theresa, it's time for you to pay."

She stared up at me, unsure of herself. I saw two things in her eyes that were at odds, despair and hope. She needed me to punish and forgive her. I thought I'd done that earlier, but maybe absolving her of the newest mystery would assuage her guilt. What else had happened to my girl to create so much self-loathing?

"Here's how this is going to work. You can share with me willingly what the fuck you were thinking and what the fuck

Bobby was referring to. Or I will beat your ass until you can't sit down for a week, right before I fuck it, and you'll still tell me what I want to know."

She was silent. She needed more from me to get her submission. I stalked to the bathroom and grabbed a wooden bath brush. Her eyes dilated when she saw it. I sat down on the edge of the bed and pulled her over my lap. I placed one of my legs over hers to keep her locked in place.

"Last chance, bella." I raised the brush and brought it down with a crack. She yelped but didn't move. I slammed the brush down again and again. "Is this what you need, Theresa? To relieve you of your guilt and self-loathing, for being a bad girl. You know you were a bad girl, don't you?" I punctuated each word with a smack.

She was squirming and crying. Her ass was still beet read from our pre-dinner belt time. With the mention of bad girl, I felt her denial. She needed to get past the denial stage.

"Come on, T, tell me what a bad girl you are." I added a little more force to my swats on her steaming backside. I felt her shiver and let go. A dozen more and she was crying like a baby, letting go of all the guilt. At least, I hoped so.

"I'm sorry," she sobbed. "I was bad. I am bad, Jimmy; you should hate me. What did I do? I did a stupid thing; I always do stupid things." I rubbed her ass; she had raised welts at her sit spot that would give her grief for days. I brought the brush down for two hard strokes. "I forgave you earlier. What's this about, Theresa?"

"I'm a bad person, Jimmy. You shouldn't leave your daughter with me," she cried. I brought the brush down several more times. This was getting me nowhere. She had to confess what was eating her up inside.

"You're right, Theresa; you are bad, a very bad girl." I spanked her again. "I guess I should cut you loose while I still can." She wailed so loudly, I was beginning to worry. "Jimmy, I did it. I did what Maggie did, after you left."

Shit. I didn't know if I could hear this confession without putting my fist through a wall. "A few months after you left and my daily episodes with those disgusting boys didn't seem to have an end in sight, I went online and got a Twitter account. I made friends with a guy. I was fourteen and full of myself and acted like I knew everything. I set up a time to meet him at the field, the same field as today."

Her voice cracked, fresh tears leaking from her beautiful eyes. "I had a bad feeling, so instead of waiting by the bleachers like he'd said, I hid behind the bushes by the washrooms. I was expecting a fifteen-year-old, a Jimmy look alike. It was an older man who arrived in a van. I watched him until he left the park. Then I ran home and cried for being such an idiot and swore I'd never tell anyone. But, one night, Bobby got me drunk and I told him about it. I never thought I would see him again. But then, today," she stopped as if to brace herself for the next part of her confession, "he was there. It was the man you saw today, Jimmy. He remembered me and called me by my name."

Damn it, I'd left, and her world fell apart in every way. I was an asshole.

"I'm bad. I'm damaged, Jimmy. When I saw that fake profile on Maggie's phone, I went dark. I don't know how else to explain it. I shut down, and another part of me took over. I thought about it in the shower. I don't even know how I got through the day without tossing my cookies. I didn't recognize that Theresa; there must be something wrong with me."

I held her and rubbed her while she cried. "Cara, you have it all wrong. You are good; this is all my fault. You needed me, and I wasn't there for you. This guy, and Steve, were reflections of me; that is why you got hurt. You needed your

Jimmy, and he wasn't there. I love you, vita mia. Please forgive me for being the worst friend and a selfish ass."

She turned around on my lap so she could wrap her legs around my waist and rest her face on my chest. I crooned in Italian as I rocked her. Minutes passed, when I felt her grip on me lessen. Her breathing changed; she'd fallen asleep.

I stood up, hanging onto her with one hand, while, with the other, I pulled back the blankets. I put her in bed and climbed in behind her. As I pulled her in tight, she sighed and pressed her ass back into my groin. In the morning, I would take her ass as I promised. But tonight, I would hold her tight and keep her safe.

I knew now what her dual look from earlier meant. If I hadn't accepted her, the despair would have won out and maybe for good. The other, hope, she now hung onto. I would feed that in her and help her to let go of all the condemnation she held over herself. I would help her rebuild and keep her safe.

Chapter 9

Jimmy

I woke long before Theresa, but instead of getting up, I stayed and held her close. When I felt her stir, I reached down and squeezed her ass. She let out the cutest mewl. Her ass was still swollen and hot from last night. I squeezed hard, and she let out a yelp. Now I had her attention. With one hand, I continued to squeeze, and with the other, I reached between her legs, stroking her silky folds.

"Theresa," I whispered, "this is mine." I squeezed her ass firmly, eliciting another yelp. My cock grew hard from the wonderful sounds she was making. She liked it a little rough. Her nether lips were wet, swollen and aroused. "This," I said, sliding my finger into her ass, "is also mine."

She squealed. "This," I plunged three digits into her sopping pussy, "is mine." I slid those same three fingers into her mouth. "This is mine, too, now suck." The vibration of her moans on my fingers made my cock throb with need. I pulled her top leg up high and slid my hard cock into her sodden folds.

"Oh," she gasped. I wrapped my arm around her thigh, creating leverage, and began pumping, slamming her swollen ass with my pelvis. The sounds she made were moving me faster toward my orgasm than I wanted, and she was on the threshold of hers. "No, T, no coming unless I say so."

"Oh, Jimmy, please, please may I come?" Music to my ears. "Now," I cried. She screeched my name as her juices coated my cock. I fucked her harder, and within seconds, she was ready to come again. "Please, Jimmy, please!"

"Are you a good girl, Theresa?"

No answer. "Say you're a good girl, and I'll let you come."

"I'm a good girl, Jimmy."

"Then, come, good girl." And she did, her vaginal walls squeezing and pulsing continually in one long orgasm. The continued contractions set me off, and within seconds, I yelled my release, filling her up. I slid out a few minutes later and pulled her tight against me.

"Theresa, last night, your confession, I need you to know that you are cleansed, free of everything that happened to you in my absence. It's my fault. I claimed you as mine when I spanked you in the treehouse, and then I left. I can't take it away, but I can spend the rest of my life trying to make up for it."

She sighed and pressed her warm ass into my groin. "Do you understand what I'm saying?"

"I love you, Jimmy," she said simply.

I kissed the back of her neck. "I love you, too, but if I have to ask again, I will restripe that fine ass of yours."

"Yes, Jimmy, I understand. I feel released. It's hard to explain, but I've always been hard on myself. With what happened yesterday, being in Maggie's shoes, I realized that I was so young. What did I know? Nothing, really. It's not my fault; I was a victim of a stalker, and it's not your fault, either.

It's not anyone's fault; it just happened. And getting to that place is really good for me. But, Jimmy?"

"Yeah, baby?"

"Honestly, I still don't know much. I've only had sex with two guys, and I don't date, have never dated. I'm a recluse, too. I'm socially awkward, and I hide from social pressure. I know I'm a premier blogger, so that doesn't make sense. But I only share what I want, and how and when I want. Social media can be a good place to hide; most people don't realize that. You're like the opposite of me; you're good at everything. Are you okay with that, with not trying to change me, accepting me just as I am? Because if you're thinking my being as I am is as a result of what's happened to me and you want to fix it, then I don't want to go any further with you. I wish to be fully accepted as I am; can you do that?"

My God, she was sweet. She could have railed against me, blamed me, but instead, she asked for acceptance. The thought had crossed my mind more than once that she had changed, that maybe she did need my help in getting to her real self. I still believed that to a degree, but it was not about changing her, it was about true acceptance so she could grow.

She could believe in herself; that's what had been taken from her. Would that help her position of solidarity? I had no idea and didn't care either way. Her, fully engaged in what she wanted out of life was all I wanted, and to share the journey with her, of course.

"Yes, Theresa Romano, I accept you just as you are, and you must do so, too, farfallina. I am a dominant man, as you know. I take what I want, and I don't share. Can you accept that about me?"

I squeezed her ass as I spoke for emphasis. "I will discipline you, but more importantly, I will love you, amoré, cherish you, and make love to every inch of your body so you will always know how much you mean to me."

She sighed in contentment. "Yes, Jimmy Falcone, I accept you."

"Then let's discuss what's next for us. I want us to live together, here, or your house, or my old house, or somewhere completely new, your choice. Pops spends eight months a year in Florida, and with Ma gone, well, I don't even know why we have this place, to be honest. Look at the size of the thing."

She laughed. "I understand, but it's been Maggie's home for her whole life, and I don't want that to change for her until she is ready. So I will move in here. But could you do one thing for me?"

"You name it, bella."

"Could you reinforce the treehouse? I want us to be able to go there. My best memories are at your house and in that treehouse."

Of course, I'll build you a village in the trees if you like."

She giggled. "I love the one we have. I just want to make sure that when you take me there, we don't fall through the floor." She hesitated then. "Um, maybe you should check with Maggie first? I don't want to ruin anything for her or your dynamic, and this is so new, she might find it unnerving."

I wasn't about to enable her lack of confidence into our life together. I was in control of my life and always had been. I slammed my hand down on her ass. She let out a startled yelp. I pushed her flat and rained blows down on her backside.

"Who's in charge here, T?"

"You are, Jimmy."

"Is Maggie something for you to worry about?"

"No, Sir."

"Good girl." I rubbed her scorching ass. "We have a very open policy, free communication, and if she has issues, she will let me know. But she adores you, and I know she wants you here."

She rolled onto her back to stare into my eyes, looking for

the truth of my words. Satisfied, she gave me a sexy smile. "So when do I move in, Master Jimmy?"

"How about today?"

"Today?" She suddenly sat up, looking like a deer in the headlights.

"Well why not? After I take your virginity, we have all day. We will go to your place, pack up your clothes, grab food and toiletries. Then, my cousin, Jules, she runs a cleaning service, she can get rid of what you don't want and get the place ready to be rented. What do you say?"

"Virginity?" she asked, blushing.

"Yes, virginity. I told you when you were bad and needed to be punished, I would fuck your ass. Even though you have been forgiven all, we did not get to it last night because you fell asleep. So now, farfallina, your ass is mine."

She was about to speak, so I grabbed her by the hair and plunged my tongue into her mouth, effectively shutting up her rebuttal. I pinched her nipple with my other hand, and she moaned in my mouth.

I pulled her back until she was on her hands and knees then knelt behind her and rubbed her back, interspersing the back rubs with light smacks to her ass. She arched her hot, gorgeous ass. I alternated between spanking her and playing with her clit. With my other hand, I held her hair tightly, keeping her in place. When she was mewling with need, I let go and grabbed lubricant. I rubbed my fingers from her sopping hole to the little bud opening of her anus. Then I rubbed lube all over my hard cock and pressed the head of my cock against her anus. She yelped and tried to pull away.

I grabbed her around the waist and delivered stinging blows to her backside, more because I wanted the heat to spread through her core. She wiggled and pushed, wanting my cock inside of her, but not her back entrance.

"Theresa," I hissed. "You are going to be punished, but

you will like it, little butterfly, I promise."

I pressed one finger into her tight cunt while simultaneously pressing the head of my cock into her ass. She screeched but held still. I, too, held still, giving her time to adjust to the new sensations she was experiencing.

"Listen to me now, cara. I will hold still, and you will back into me as you relax your muscles, understand?"

She nodded, which was all she seemed capable of doing. I rubbed her clit, and as I did, she arched her backside and I slid in further. It seemed to take forever to get her halfway, but I didn't lose any hardness. She was so tight and turned on, she just needed to let go of her fear.

I stroked her wet, swollen lips and then plunged all my digits inside her channel. It was the green light as she arched her back and began to move against me. In a few thrusts, I was seated fully inside her tight ass. She was beside herself with sensation and came apart within a few strokes. Then she let out a long keen as one orgasm after another ripped through her body. The intensity of the sensations she was experiencing also ripped through my own body and it wasn't long until I came in her. Exhausted, we collapsed on the bed for a few minutes, catching our breath.

"Oh my God, Jimmy, that was amazing. I had no idea anal sex could be so good. It gives new meaning to that saying 'hurts so good.'"

I laughed and pulled her up. "Okay, my little slut, shower time and breakfast, and then we'll head over to your place."

Theresa

When I came downstairs, freshly showered and feeling a bit like a boneless fish, Jimmy had an omelet ready for me laden with vegetables, no cheese and no toast, just the way I liked it. How did he know? Maybe it wasn't a matter of knowing but simply understanding my nature and the respect I held for my body.

Somehow, the man knew me, and it was as if all that time apart never occurred. That from the time he left until now could be summarized as a weird kind of limbo. Even college seemed a dream. This, our life now and our life before, seemed real.

On the drive to my house, we discussed what to do with the two houses. "Jimmy, do you think I should sell my house or rent it?"

"I spoke with Bobby while you were getting ready; he says there are a half dozen new residents coming into the hospital in the next few weeks and feels he could get your place rented out for a premium if you leave it furnished. How does that sound?"

I was surprised at how fast this was working out. "Fine. Great, actually. So, what do we need to do then?"

"I have a couple of the guys coming in two hours with a work van. Whatever you want to take, furniture wise, if anything, can be loaded. I have a bunch of empty boxes in my garage at the old house. We can fill those with whatever personal items you want. And we can use suitcases for your clothing and bags for your shoes. The food we can move over to my fridge at the old house or our place, whatever you think. That's it, really. Jules will take care of the cleaning, and Bobby volunteered to stage the house before he shows it for you to the new residents."

"Wow, I don't know what to say. You have everything so well in hand. What are your thoughts on my office, like where should I set up at your place? I definitely need an office space, and I don't want to invade yours."

"We have tons of rooms that aren't being used, but I have

one in mind I think you will really like. Later if you want to replace your office furniture, then we can store the old stuff in my garage or sell it, whatever you want. But I'd like your office to be transferable, because it will make you comfortable."

Again, I was speechless. He was so good at controlling and organizing. Something that would have taken me weeks to accomplish was being done in a day. I sat back in my seat, a smile on my face. Today was a good day. I could feel things lifting in my world, taking on a new direction and a new meaning. I was excited for the move. "Jimmy?"

"Yeah, babe?"

"Thank you. I'm grateful to you for making this process so easy for me. I feel excited and I'm really happy."

Jimmy smiled. "Me too, cara," he said, placing his hand possessively on my leg and giving it a little squeeze. "By the way, T, I saw Bobby and Josh's flat."

"Really?" Surprise laced my voice.

"I really like it. Bobby has an incredible eye. I offered him a job as his style is so in right now."

"That's crazy, really? What did he say?"

Jimmy laughed. "He's not ready to tell the hospital to beat it yet. But he would like to do some stuff for me on the side to keep up his creative flair, he said. So, he will be decorating a few apartments I have in a complex on the trendy side of town. I'm really glad I met him; he's a cool guy."

I was thrilled. "He is, and poor Josh, he will be happy that Bobby is too busy to redo their condo every four weeks."

Jimmy laughed. "Never thought of that."

We arrived at my house. Jimmy pulled me up on my tiptoes when he opened my door for me. I pressed into him, and he wrapped his arms around me. "I'm so happy, Jimmy. I love you."

"I love you, too."

Chapter 10

Theresa

Relief flooded me when Maggie returned to the house that evening, and she was happy to see me. "Theresa, Dad told me you moved in, and I want you to know I'm so okay with it."

"I'm relieved, Maggie, thank you. Now that I'm here, please ask me for help if you need anything or want to go for ice cream or anything. I really want us to be friends. And I'm hoping you are available after school for a birthday planning meeting?"

She nodded enthusiastically.

"Great, um, do you get picked up or take the bus? How does this work?"

Maggie laughed. "Tessa takes me and Ems to cheerleading practice on Mondays, because Dad is at work, then she takes me back to her place for dinner and I get picked up later. Could you come to cheerleading practice at 3:30 tomorrow? I would love it if you would come. Then we could come home together."

Wow, I was honored. "Sure. Are you allowed to use your phone?"

"I can use the phone, but that's it."

"Great, text me the address and I'll meet you there. Um, Maggie, I'm not much of a cook, but maybe you and I could get something made for your dad tomorrow as a surprise. Any ideas of something easy we could do together?"

She thought for a minute and then said, "I have the perfect idea; let's do tacos. You can brown meat, right?" It wasn't an insult; she was genuinely asking.

I nodded my head yes.

"Great, so you can do the meat and warm the shells, and I will cut up the vegetables and shred the cheese. Do you like guacamole? My dad loves it, but if you can't make homemade, you can buy some already prepared."

"What time does he usually get home?"

"It depends on if I'm eating at Em's. If he knows dinner is at home, five, probably."

"Cheerleading is an hour? Let's tell your dad dinner at six, then he doesn't have to rush, and it gives us time to shop and get back to make it. Sound good? We can talk about your birthday during dinner, and I'll make some notes and come up with a plan."

"Thanks, Theresa." She gave me a hug and said good-night. I found Jimmy in his office on the phone, speaking heatedly in Italian. I got the gist of the conversation, although I could not, by any stretch, be an interpreter. He invited me in, and I sat down in the same seat where Jimmy had brought me to his office the day of his mother's wake. Had it only been a few weeks? My life without Jimmy Falcone now felt like forever ago. He'd so completely taken over my life that the time spent between childhood and now was a blur.

He hung up the phone. "Hello, Tesoro. How did it go with Maggie? She seemed happy?"

He sat back and studied me, looking for what, exactly, I wasn't sure.

"I know you run your show, but it means a lot to me to know how she feels about this without your interference. It gives me some reference on how to move forward."

"Hmm, well, I tell you what, bella, you get naked and sit on my desk with your knees wide, and I will tell you."

I blushed. He'd caught me by surprise, but I was game, so I stood up and slowly slid down my black silk lounging pants, allowing them to puddle at my feet. Then I lifted the matching shirt over my head and tossed it in his direction. It landed directly in front of him on the desk. He grinned. I had no bra on and no underwear. His appreciative gaze made me feel sexy and turned on. I loved the way he eyed up and down my body.

This was a new sensation for me, as I used to be so embarrassed by my own nudity, I would not go to bed naked. I didn't like how I looked, didn't think how I looked was worth noticing or mentioning. But Jimmy, he made me feel like I was a goddess. He loved the way I looked. That appreciation egged me on to actions I would have never considered a few weeks ago.

I turned around and placed my ass on his desk then hooked my heels on the edges of the desk and opened my knees wide. I leaned my elbows back and dropped my head so my face was only inches from his.

He leaned down and kissed me, plunging his tongue into my mouth, capturing my tongue between his teeth, nipping at me.

I was wet. I could feel the juices soaking my crease.

Jimmy stood up, releasing my mouth and coming around the desk to the front. He sat down on the chair I'd vacated and pulled it forward so he could lean his face between my thighs. His hot breath sent a shudder through my body. I was so ready to be taken. He blew his hot breath on my apex and drew one finger from my slit to my anus. Next, he pressed his thumb into my ass and licked my pussy.

I arched up into his mouth trying to get closer, get him deeper.

"Theresa, are you my little slut?" His words sparked a pulse deep within me that resulted in another shudder. He plunged a finger into my vagina and another into my ass. "Theresa, answer me, are you my little slut?"

"Yes, Jimmy."

"Good girl." He spanked my mons. "Now turn around with your knees and hands on my desk." As I did, he went to his desk drawer and pulled out a nasty looking wooden ruler. My expression must have shown my reluctance to feel it on my backside, because Jimmy's gaze changed from dominant to predator. The shift was subtle, but it was a shift all the same that I now knew indicated a new sexual experience.

He stayed in front of me but lowered back to his office chair to look me in the eyes. "This, Tesoro, is for girls who need correction. Do you need correction, Theresa?"

I shook my head vigorously no.

He laughed. "We'll see."

He moved behind me and plunged a finger into my sopping pussy, because despite my fear of the ruler, the very idea of it turned me on. He sank another digit into my ass and began pumping in and out of both. I arched and moaned piteously, looking for release. His other hand began to rain slaps on my backside. The kaleidoscope of sensations sent me off the edge, and I came hard.

Jimmy kept his fingers in until my orgasm subsided. "Tsk, tsk, bella. Did you come without asking permission?"

Shit! "Um, uh, yes?"

I heard him chuckle. "Yes, you did, Tesoro. You have been naughty and need reminding of your position." I felt the ruler come down on my backside with a crack. I jumped, gasping in surprise. But before I could process the sting on my right cheek, it came down again on my left and then in such quick succession, all I could do was try to maintain position.

He lifted me off the desk and placed me on the chaise lounge he had in his office, then he took off his belt and wrapped it around my wrists. I was on my knees, my fists behind me and pressed into my lower back. I had no momentum to change my position, even if I wanted to. Jimmy was behind me, and I couldn't see what he was doing, could only hear sounds and try to decipher what was going to happen next.

My stinging backside hurt like crazy, but I was so turned on, I could feel my soaking slit peering at Jimmy, open and exposed and wanting some action. I had learned my lesson; I would not come again without permission. Jimmy left the room and was back a few minutes later. He slid something into my ass.

"Ah, Tesoro, you should see the beautiful sight you make. Just seeing you trussed up like this in my office makes me want to fuck you until you scream."

I felt my lady parts clench. Oh God, he was making me hot, burning hot. "Jimmy, what did you put in my ass? It's hot!" I began to twist and moan and try to get up, to dislodge the item in my ass that was making me so uncomfortable.

"It's called figging. I have a ginger plug in your ass. Now be a good girl and stay still while I create more burning heat. If you're good, I will fuck you until the burn is gone." Then I felt a crack across my sit spot. The heat from the ruler and from the ginger was creating a wanton mess in my lady parts. I wanted to scream. I wanted to jump in a lake, get fucked by an entire football team, the sensations were driving me insane.

He repeated the spanking until I lost count and became a mewling, begging mess. Then I felt his red-hot cock at the entrance to my folds, and I cried with relief. "Yes, yes, yes, please," I begged. Jimmy took me in one thrust and it was all I could do to not come. Jimmy banged me hard, and with each slam of his pelvis, the ginger moved and created more heat.

"Please, I beg of you, take it out, Jimmy, please, I can't take anymore."

Jimmy kept up the pounding from behind, but he reached around and pinched my clitoris and said, "Come!"

I did, my orgasm accompanied by a long keen, a primordial release of the kind I'd never felt before. In that moment of release, my life flashed before me, my birth, my existence. I screamed with the intensity and orgasmed again and again, cresting and falling. I lost sense of time and space. It was only when I felt my arms being released that I started my descent back to earth.

"Good girl, Tesoro." I could barely smile, and my eyes drooped. Jimmy scooped me up and carried me to the bed. I was asleep the moment he put me down, not even twitching when he wiped me and pulled the blankets over me. I sank into a deep slumber.

Jimmy

My God, she was amazing; she was made for me, for my cock and for my kink. Theresa was perfect. I understood why I'd fallen so hard for her when we were kids. Somehow, my dominant self had recognized her submissive self, even in our friendship as children.

I pictured her as a little girl, her enormous blue eyes looking at me with pure love and trust. She had trusted me with her life back then. I didn't have that with her yet. I would win it back; it would just take time, mostly, by letting go of things that were no longer part of her life. Her primal scream had set something off in me. It awoke in me a sense of conviction, the desire to create and control. Being with her took away the sense of burden I'd felt these past few years, running the company. Not just the company, but keeping our Sicilian connections at bay. My pa was old school; he didn't see a problem with using his connections, where I preferred to use my degree and my head.

He put me in charge of everything when my ma got sick two years ago. Since then, I have been slowly changing the direction of the company. It's not as if we engaged in illegal activities, we didn't, but for my pops, his idea of business had been to line the pockets of anyone who said no or got in our way. That wasn't my way, but occasionally, I'd be hard pressed to follow the legitimate path. That was where my challenges would come, and I would choose the path less followed, while I looked for ways to appease everyone.

The toll it was taking on me was what I'd been struggling with when Theresa had walked through the front door. She inspired me to be better, to do better, to be the Jimmy who was truthful, loving, kind, protective, to seek happiness and love to play and be with my family. She gave me my life back, just her existence, who she was and what she represented. I would guard that like the treasure I knew it to be.

Tonight, she never questioned me. She had total faith in me that I would follow through on my promise, and I did. Now, with both my girls safely tucked away, I went back to my earlier conversation with my father.

He was sending my second cousin to Philly. He had flown into Florida from Italy. After spending some time together, my pops decided that he needed to come to Philadelphia and be part of our company. We'd see. I didn't recall ever meeting this cousin, and as I'd said, I wasn't into old school business tactics. If this kid was legitimate, then finding a place for him was not a problem, but if he proved to be anything but, back to Italy or wherever the fuck he wanted, but not here, and not with my company.

The next morning as Maggie and I were heading out the door, Theresa said she would be picking Maggie up from cheerleading and would have dinner ready for 6:00 pm. That was perfect; I was picking up my cousin from the airport at 5:00. I would bring him back for dinner and get to know him. "I'm bringing a guest, Tesoro; see you at 6:00." Then Mags and I were out the door.

Theresa

Being in Jimmy's kitchen was a little overwhelming, but it did remind me of dinner, so I made a list and looked up how to make guacamole. I was determined to make this dinner from scratch, with homemade salsa and guacamole.

At 2:30, I hit the grocery store, and just as I was packing the groceries in my car, the awaited text from Maggie came through. Pulling out of the store parking lot, I wondered how Jimmy was doing. He'd been strangely quiet today, whereas, usually, he texted me several times to see what I was doing or wearing; sometimes we had phone sex. Today, just a quick, *be good, I'm busy, see you at 6:00 with Joseph.*

I was excited watching Maggie's practice; the team was excellent, and Tessa was a great coach. I started writing notes on my tablet and decided I would do a post on cheerleading as a sport and as a support for team sports. Emma was, by far, the best cheerleader on the team. She did gymnastics, and you could tell.

Maggie took dance so rhythmically, she moved the best, but the big moves were all Emma. It was nice that the two friends could be so close and have such different skill sets yet have no jealousy. I imagined it was the excellent parenting and friendship both girls had.

The rest of the team seemed less dedicated but performed well. I couldn't believe the type of draw cheerleading had. I didn't even remember if our school had offered cheerleading, that was how far off the radar it had been just ten years ago.

Maggie and I chattered away happily while preparing dinner. We both changed our clothing after the messy stuff was done, and she opened the wine for dinner. I found Maggie to be one of the most independent almost-thirteen-year-olds I'd ever met. Living with Jimmy, he taught her a lot about independence, while Maria had taught her how to navigate the kitchen like a pro. She could cook almost as well as her father. I was soon overpowered by her capabilities and stayed with frying the meat and heating the shells; she made everything else.

I heard the front door open and two voices, one deeper, Jimmy's, and one with a heavy Italian accent. That must be the cousin. They entered the dining room from the living room side while Maggie and I entered from the kitchen and almost collided with each other.

"Daddy," Maggie burst out as she moved into him for a hug.

I smiled. I loved how close they were and how happy they were to see each other. I felt eyes watching and glanced from the happy duo to Joseph. He wasn't looking at them, though; he was watching me. His expression was predatory, much like Jimmy's, but where Jimmy's was playful, this guy's was sinister.

My eyes grew wide, a sliver of fear racing up my spine. He smiled, and it was anything but warm. I would have to be careful around this one. I knew already his intentions, and they were not honorable. Jimmy released Maggie and turned to me. I quickly painted a different expression on my face. Jimmy frowned but said nothing.

Maggie and I brought in the food from the kitchen, setting everything up buffet style in the center of the table while the guys got themselves drinks. Joseph commented on the house and the furnishings constantly. I got the sense that his interests lay strictly in money and acquisitions.

We sat down to eat. "Thank you, ladies, for the wonderful meal," Jimmy said when he'd finished. He stood and started clearing.

Joseph's eyes nearly bugged out of his head. "Doing women's work, Jimmy?" he sneered.

Jimmy carried himself very nonchalantly, but I could tell he was angry. "I know what you are used to in Sicily, but around here, I love and honor the women in my life, just as they love and honor me. Dishes aren't women's work, Joe; it is just work. I think you need a lesson in American standards. Come, you can help me."

Joe looked like he was going to reject when Jimmy's eyes turned to steel. Joe got up and grabbed our dishes.

When they left the room, Maggie and I laughed behind our hands.

"If he's going to hang around with my dad, he's got a lot to learn."

I nodded in agreement. "Come on, Maggie, let's go sit outside and go over your birthday party. I have some ideas." I grabbed my tablet and the two of us scooted outside. "So, what are your thoughts on using the pool and having a water fantasy pool party?"

"Oh, I like it," she said, her eyes lighting up. "Does that mean that we need costumes, or is there a color theme?"

I grinned at her enthusiasm and replied, "I was thinking black and pink. Also, have you heard of Rachel Hunt?"

"Who hasn't?" Maggie said. "She is the hottest iron chef on television. Dad and I watch her show sometimes."

"I know Rachel and her partner, Sam. I'm going to have them design the teen fantasy pool party menu. How does that sound?"

"Seriously, oh my God, Theresa, yes!" she practically screeched.

I was putting out ideas to see where her thoughts were gravitating. She seemed super excited about Rachel and the food; maybe I would work on the party theme and come up with more ideas. "So, listen, I heard there are state championships coming up? Have you heard of the Junior Jaguars?"

Maggie was literally bouncing up and down in her seat. "Yes, they won the championship last year, and they are from Philadelphia."

I smiled. "That's right. Well, I have it on good authority that Tessa is good friends with their coach. Would you be interested in having them come here and perform for your birthday?"

Her face dropped. "No, I don't think so; they will be a reminder of how bad we are, and the guys will think they're hot instead of us."

I sucked at this. I decided to take a different track. "How many people do you want to invite? I was thinking fifty in total, half boys and half girls?"

"Oh, that many, do you think my dad will be okay with that?"

"Your dad said the sky's the limit, as many as you want."

Maggie's eyes danced. "Well, then, fifty sounds perfect, but not the split. I can't think of more than twenty boys I'd want at my house." She giggled.

I joined her and that was when Jimmy and Joe joined us on the deck. Jimmy brought out dessert coffees and treats. I accepted the coffee, but not the treats.

"Whatsa matter, Theresa, afraid your hips will get wider?" Joe laughed. The three of us looked at Joe like he was from another planet. Before Jimmy or I could say anything, Maggie said, "Theresa is perfect. I wish I had her hips."

That shut Joe up and effectively ended our planning session. We got onto safe, generic topics about travel and weather. Maggie removed herself and headed off to do her homework. I was going to follow her lead, but I got a silent shake from Jimmy. He didn't want to get stuck with this guy. I didn't blame him.

It was hard seeing any familial connection at all. Jimmy was my blond, Italian giant, while Joe was my height and built like a bull. I guess he could be considered attractive, but he certainly wasn't my type. He was exactly what I pictured in a Sicilian from the old country. After an hour or so longer, Jimmy said it was time. He was taking Joe to a set of rooms his father had rented for him downtown, so he'd be closer to the action.

When Jimmy returned, he found me in bed reading. He flopped down and ran his hands over his face as if to wash away his day. I put my book down and moved beside him, resting my head on his chest.

"Tough day, Sir?"

He liked my use of 'Sir' and a smile lit up his face. He rolled toward me, catching my chin in his hand. "It was, Tesoro, but it's all done now. There is only me and you and what I've been dreaming of doing to you all day."

My lady parts squeezed and did a cheer. I had been dreaming of things all day as well. I went to the closet, telling Jimmy to close his eyes. When I emerged, I was wearing a cheerleading outfit that Tessa had loaned me with a wink and a giggle.

I struck a pose and told him to open his eyes. He roamed

my body, his eyes glittering. "T, how did you know I was dreaming of fucking a cheerleader tonight?"

I winked. "I know everything, Jimmy Falcone, everything there is to know about you."

"Then you know what I'm thinking right now." I gulped at the look of desire in his eyes. I walked to him and knelt at his feet, undid his zipper and pulled out his hard cock, putting his length in my mouth.

He moaned and lay back on the bed. "Oh, baby, getting sucked off by the hottest cheerleader is a dream come true."

Chapter 11

Theresa

I was so nervous. Fellow blogger and queen of the cooking channel, Rachel Hunt would be here any moment to discuss the menu for Maggie's birthday. I answered the door and invited Rachel and Sam in. We'd only met in person once at a benefit, and I was not a conversation carrier at all.

She was so enthralled with Jimmy's gourmet kitchen, she asked if she could make everything here and film it for her show. I quickly texted Jimmy while she and Sam wandered around my kitchen oohing and awing about every little thing.

> *(Me) Help! "Scream emoji"*
> *(Jimmy) What's wrong, baby, miss me?*
> *(Me) Yes, but the problem is Rachel Hunt. I need help,*
>   *please can you come?*
> *(Jimmy) see you in 5*

I heaved a sigh of relief. Jimmy could navigate these two women like it was nobody's business. Just as they made their way to the gourmet, double turbo air, double section fridges, Jimmy walked through the door. He came into the kitchen, saw the ladies, saw me dying in a pool of doubt and turned into suave Jimmy.

"Buongiorno, bellissima signore," he said, taking each of their hands and kissing them. "Welcome to my humble abode." Jimmy was wearing jeans that were tight enough to outline his powerful legs. Added to that were black boots and a black t-shirt that offset his olive coloring and blond surfer hair. He looked like he'd stepped out of a fantasy.

Both women blushed.

"Rachel Hunt, I love your recipes; my daughter and I watch your show. I'm honored." He kissed her hand again and then finally let it go. It was funny seeing Rachel speechless. Jimmy gracefully continued to lead the conversation. "I hear you are lending your expertise for my daughter's thirteenth birthday. I cannot tell you enough how thrilled I am to have you and your lovely assistant here in my home."

Rachel seemed to gain control of herself. Her panties were probably soaked. I snickered; Jimmy had that effect on women. "Oh, Mr. Falcone, I mentioned to Theresa that we would love to film an episode of my show here while preparing the food for the birthday. I do hope it is allowed?"

Now he knew why I called him. I wasn't about to let a film crew in his home if he didn't want one. I held my breath while he deliberated. Then I watched as he threw in a parameter of his own. "Oh, bella, I'm sure Maggie would love to participate in your show. She would be thrilled to be sharing this portion of her birthday party with the world. What do you say, T, wouldn't Maggie love that?"

"She would, but I think only if she had Emma with her."

"Ah, bella," he said, kissing me deeply, "you think of everything. Of course, the best friend must be in attendance, right, Samantha?"

Sam, who had not spoken a word since Jimmy had waltzed into the kitchen, said, "Yes, Mr. Falcone, of course."

It was now up to Rachel. If she wanted to film here, she would have two guest assistants. "I don't see why we couldn't. It's a deal, Mr. Falcone."

"Jimmy," he said, "please call me Jimmy, bella."

I watched Rachel—she was turned on.

"I must leave you beautiful women in the hands of my capable and lovely Theresa. Enjoy your day," he said as he headed out the door.

The three of us sat down and, over coffee, finalized the menu, deciding on pizza pinwheels, spicy potato skins with bean dip, wings, truffle, mini cheese cake, chocolate dipped fruit, and a do it yourself burger bar with vegetable ranch cups. The episode would be *Party Food for Teens*. I couldn't wait to tell Maggie. With what I considered the hard part out of the way, I thought about entertainment and spent the rest of my day solidifying plans.

The day of the filming, Jimmy stayed home to help me set up the decorations as the party started at noon the next day and went until 8:00 pm. Maggie and Emma had their makeup and hair done by Rachel Hunt's crew, their outfits chosen, and were ready to shoot the cooking show.

Jimmy and I went outside, filling three hundred pink and black balloons. Then we put them in netting that Jimmy rigged to fall when the cord was pulled. Next, we set up the food tables, the tiki bar and the base for the DIY rotating burger bar.

We finished all of that and hung the twenty-five lanterns I'd purchased with pink candles in the center. Some we hung on poles around the pool, and others we set around the food area with a few over by the loungers.

When the show finished filming, around the same time we were done, Tessa took the girls home for dinner and a sleepover, so Jimmy and I could finish the surprise portion of Maggie's birthday. Jimmy and Al were making a stage and setting it up in the backyard for the band I'd hired.

Maggie and Emma hugged me before they left. "Thanks, Theresa, that was the coolest," they said and headed out the door.

With the girls out of the way, Jimmy and Al went to town on the stage. It was eight by the time we finished everything and Al left.

"Theresa, I'm going to take you out for dinner, farfallina. You have had a busy day, my love. I'm thinking Gino's for steak; what do you think?"

"Mmm, meat sounds good. I need the extra iron to keep me energized," I said, reaching my arms up and circling them around him.

He kissed me deeply and I felt it right down to my toes. "Maybe we don't need dinner," I moaned.

Jimmy pulled away, laughing.

"You're too skinny already. Into the shower with you."

I decided to play the brat and said, "No I don't think so; you can't make me."

His eyes lit up like a kid at Christmas. "No?"

"Uh-uh," I said, shaking my head, "and you can't make me." I laughed then took off like a shot. My sweaty Hercules caught up to me at the stairwell and threw me over his shoulder, spanking my ass up the staircase and down the hall.

When we got to our suite, he threw me on the bed then reached down and ripped my track pants off. I squealed in surprise. He grabbed my ankles and flipped me over, peppering my backside with hard slaps.

"I can't, farfallina? Make you obey? Are you sure?" He increased the intensity, and now I was questioning the wisdom of my actions. He continued to rain down the blows, paying special attention to my sit spot.

I tried to get away, but he kept me pressed into the bed. He suddenly spanked my mons, and I screeched. "No fair," I whined.

"I'll do it again, unless you ask me nicely not to."

Before I could ask, he did it again, and again I screeched, but this time, wetness splayed over my inner thighs with the slap. Despite my protestations, his pussy slaps were turning me on.

"I see my little slut likes the rough housing," he said as he slapped my ass and my mons repeatedly until I orgasmed with much intensity. He hadn't even put a single finger inside of me; this was all from spanking.

He pulled off his sweat pants in record time and plunged into me with his hard cock while continuing to spank me.

I cried out, "Yes, Jimmy, yes, don't stop. Ah, oh God! Jimmy!" I came like there was no tomorrow.

He shuddered and trembled on his release, his breath coming out in a long, hissing moan. He collapsed on the bed beside me.

"Now, I really need that steak," I said, trembling as I tried to stand.

Jimmy laughed, and it was into the shower for us both. He picked me up and carried me. When the hot water hit my ass, I yelped and quickly turned around. But Jimmy turned me back, and as the spray hit me, he plunged his fingers in and out, bringing me to orgasm two more times.

I slunk against him in the shower. I felt thoroughly fucked. Jimmy washed my hair while I leaned into him, pressing my face into his chest and feeling the strength of his body as he helped to support and clean me up.

When we were done, he threw on jeans and a dress shirt. I chose a tight, black number with my wedges and put my hair up in a messy bun. We were out the door in ten minutes, both of us starving. Gino was happy to see us. I'd gone to school with his sister, and he'd played Sunday football with Jimmy when he wasn't too busy with the restaurant.

We had Chianti and Caprese salads to start.

"So, what do you think of the backyard so far? Do you think Maggie will like it?" I asked.

"Maggie will love it, trust me. She's never had anything like this before, T. You know my ma, love went into everything she did, but she was not showy. She kept everything simple, like she did with our birthdays growing up."

"It's funny you mention that. I often wonder why you moved into such a large palatial house. It is the exact opposite of her taste."

Our steaks had arrived. Jimmy was taking his first bite when he stopped and said, "I have wondered the same thing. I don't think ma liked the house. Pa liked it; he always likes things to look a certain way."

James senior was a different duck, totally old school. I wondered if the move had anything to do with me. Maybe he didn't think I was Falcone material. "Jimmy, when you last spoke with your father, did you mention that I had moved in?"

Jimmy was chewing his steak, his look thoughtful. "Yes, I did. What are you thinking, Theresa?"

"Well, this is just a thought, but after you told him, how long did it take for him to tell you that he wanted you to bring Joe into the business and get him set up?"

Jimmy pushed his plate away and picked up his wine glass, taking a long sip. "Right after I told him you'd moved in."

"I'm not sure what's going on, Jimmy, but has your father ever sent anyone over from the old country with this type of request before? Maybe your father has someone in mind for you, and I'm not it. Maybe, like yourself, he saw where the relationship was going, or could go, and headed it off by moving his family out of the old neighborhood?"

I downed my wine while I waited for him to process and

respond to me. Maybe I was paranoid, but my thoughts strayed to another scenario. What if the accident that had caused the death of Maggie's mother and her date was no accident? I wanted to slap myself for having such a horrid thought and the corresponding expression that I couldn't hide in time from Jimmy.

"What are you thinking, Theresa? Just say it."

"I don't want to, Jimmy. I'll sound paranoid; the thought I had seems ridiculous."

"Theresa, whatever it is, you can say it. Let me decide how crazy it sounds."

I sighed and took a big sip of wine.

"Jimmy, what if everything that has happened has been to make you exactly what you are, what if your father moved you before you could consider that early marriage, before you could get me pregnant? He had other plans for you. What if Christina's accident was not an accident, what if that was another way for your father to gain control of you and the factors surrounding you? Having custody of Maggie, letting your mother raise her. You'd have nothing else to focus on but the company."

He was silent, and I was afraid I'd overstepped. I started to apologize, but he held up his hand to stop me.

"T, what you say, it doesn't sound crazy. I'd like to think my old man has enough respect for me that no matter what I did in my private life, he knew I would never screw up the family business, but you could be right. With my ma gone, so is the more humane part of his personality. If he wants you gone, maybe Joe is a plant. I certainly didn't like the way he was looking at you, and the circumstances surrounding Christina's death don't fit. It seemed odd, although, at the time, I didn't question it. But I do know it wasn't raining, and it was early evening."

He thought a minute then went on, "The police report

said it was raining and late, close to midnight, and that they'd been drinking. I don't know about Kevin, her boyfriend, but I know Christina wasn't a drinker. The tox screen confirmed what the cop said, that there were high levels of alcohol. Hmm, maybe we can talk to Josh and see if he can use his connections to dig up that file, maybe talk to the cop who wrote the report. If it leads nowhere, then maybe we are both being paranoid. But if there has been tampering, I want to know."

I shuddered, feeling suddenly vulnerable. Could it be? Could James Senior really be that man who did those types of things?

"Come, bella, let's go home; we have a long day tomorrow."

I nodded. We said goodnight to Gino and left.

Jimmy

I held Theresa in my arms. She was shaking when we got into bed. Sleep eluded me as I turned events over and over again in my mind. Could my pops really be that guy? He had come over from the old country, and he had been involved in shady dealings in my younger years; I knew that. The mansion I was sleeping in was a result of a spike in our company's growth, but despite my digging, I'd never found what caused the spike.

The more I thought on it, the more what T had said made sense. My dad, the kingpin, staging all sorts of events to suit his needs? His wants? What was his plan with Joe? Why send him now? I had many questions for which there were no immediate answers. When sleep finally claimed me, I was determined to get answers, and it would begin with Josh.

Chapter 12

Jimmy

Al and Bobby arrived early to help me and T set up the birthday girl's dream party. Tessa would be bringing the girls in an hour to meet up with Rachel to have hair, wardrobe and makeup done to film the birthday menu reaction in our kitchen. Theresa guzzled down two cups of espresso and was about to start a third before I took her cup away. "Don't be so nervous, farfallina. Everything will be perfect."

She nodded and headed outside to join Bobby. She was stressing, but I wasn't. Everything was in place. Al and I were hanging the twinkle lights for the stage. It was good to have just the two of us together. Al's father, Alphonse, had worked for my father since the beginning, and Al, who was four years my senior, had been with the company since high school, working weekends and fulltime in the summer.

I wanted to feel him out about my thoughts without sharing them. Who knew, maybe Al, my best friend, was a

Dad-plant as well. As we stood untangling the lights, I glanced over at Theresa. She and Bobby had just finished blowing up thirteen inflatable pink flamingos and thirteen black penguin floaties for the pool. They were laughing about something, causing me to smile.

"What's up, boss?"

"Just watching T; Bobby has her laughing about something, and I love watching her laugh."

Al smiled. "She's a good person, Jimmy. I remember her as a kid; she was a cutie, even back then. You sure were smitten with her. Still are, I guess, eh?"

"Back then she was just a cute little girl without a mother, and with a father who was never around. She needed someone; I just happened to be that someone."

He nodded. "Yep and your ma loved her, always doting on her, probably because she had no girls of her own."

Here was my chance to dig a bit. "Yep, Ma sure seemed attached, but not Pops. He always seemed to look at her as a nuisance."

I didn't think that; it was a test to see what, if anything, Al knew. "Yeah, he was always griping to my pops about you marking your territory way too young to know what the hell you were doing. I guess you proved them wrong, eh, boss?"

It was such an innocent statement; one I would have thought nothing of two days ago. But things had changed, and I was determined to find out what was really going on. "Yeah," I said lightly. "That's probably why he moved us, to get me away from making what he thought was a mistake."

I waited for Al's response. It was long in coming, but he finally said, "Yeah, Jimmy. I think so, too." That was enough for now. Enough to start asking questions and see what I could discover.

Theresa

I felt like the to do list was growing, not getting smaller. Every time I did something, I remembered three other things that needed to be done. At this rate, I would be a pile of mush in no time. I saw Jimmy from across the lawn. He and Al had done the stage, and it looked amazing. I gave them the thumbs up.

Jimmy had an outdoor bar already in place. We covered it with bamboo to give it a tiki bar feel and added a cover that said Maggie's Tiki Bar. With that done last night, Bobby and I needed to stock the bar with mix and ice as we were offering virgin blended drinks, like Piña Coladas, Margaritas, and Bellinis, or just pop, juice, or water. We brought out packages of drink umbrellas, fresh fruit for decoration, and moved the bar stools. Standing back to admire our handy work, I was thrilled with how authentic it looked.

As we finished, Rachel and the girls opened the kitchen door to indicate the filming was completed. "Thank you, Rachel, once again for your help in making this day special."

Rachel's response was flippant until Jimmy made his appearance. Then she was all smiles and flutters. I rolled my eyes as Jimmy walked her and the crew out the front and turned my attention to Maggie.

"Theresa, I'm so nervous. What if people don't show up? What if the party isn't cool? What if my friends don't have fun?"

I tried not to laugh; it wasn't her I found amusing, but the teenage angst. I remember Jimmy being like her when the family would host an event in his honor. "Listen up, chicklet. Fifty invites went out and forty-eight confirmations came back. This is going to be the party of the year. The tiki bar will be a hit, and there is non-stop action planned, games, fun and a ton of food. And most importantly, the secret band. Stop worrying. Leave that to me."

Her large doe eyes softened. "Thank you for doing this. You're right. It's going to be the party of the year."

"That's the spirit. Now you and Ems change into your beach outfits. I left a present on your bed."

She squealed in excitement and took off with Emma right on her heels.

Jimmy was suddenly at my side. "T, you are incredible! This is incredible! My back yard never looked like so much fun. You may have to organize my party, Tesoro."

"Well, I put on a brave face for her, but seriously, Jimmy, what if she's right and it bombs? It will be all my fault. I wish I had time for a spanking."

His eyes lit up. "You do? Tell me why, bella."

"The stress relief I get is better than any drug, but I'm sure you knew that already."

He squeezed my ass. "I do, but I like hearing you say it."

Suddenly, fifteen kids came pouring into the backyard.

"Oh, God, Jimmy, its begun; please don't leave me." I was seriously freaking out.

"I won't leave you, Tesoro. I will be manning the tiki bar. Come and have a drink anytime you like; I have a few things set aside for the adults." As the kids headed over to the tiki bar for drinks, I made some last minute fussing. To keep everyone organized, I had purchased a large wicker basket for each kid with their name on it, and included was their party favor, which consisted of a towel in either pink or black, goggles, and a mini suntan lotion.

Once the kids had their drinks, I took them over to the line of baskets, so they could keep their personal belongings safe. Then I headed inside to grab the snacks. Tessa helped me, and when we came outside and made the rounds with our loaded trays, the number of kids had doubled. I was getting many '*thank you, Mrs. Falcone,*' and '*great spread, Mrs. F.*'

I guess they assumed I was Maggie's mother. I was inside grabbing more snacks, when Maggie came downstairs wearing her present. A hot pink one-piece bathing suit, with black heels and a matching black wrap. With her hair and makeup professionally done, and the black sunglasses, Maggie looked like a child supermodel.

"Oh my God, Mags, you're a knock out; those poor boys."

She giggled and blushed. "You really think so, T?"

"Like yeah, your dad's going to kill me." She looked seventeen and a total knock out. She deserved an entrance. I beckoned her to the doorway and told her to wait. I ran up to the stage and grabbed the microphone. "Ladies and gentlemen, I present to you the birthday girl, Maggie Falcone." She strutted out the door with Em right behind her.

When Maggie Falcone stepped outside, every person stopped what they were doing, and jaws dropped.

"See that, Mags," I said, whispering in her ear after getting off the stage. "You are the goddess today; work it, and you'll slay them."

She had a Jimmy glint in her eye as she set off to greet her guests. By the time she reached the pool, she had every boy at the party surrounding her. I was so excited to watch her. Today, she let the full Maggie shine, no hesitation, no holding back; she worked the party like a pro, reminding me so much of her dad.

As Tessa and I carried food out, I kept hearing '*your parents are so cool, Maggie, this is awesome,*' the girls telling her how hot she looked. Every kid had something positive they were sharing and that was all I needed to hear. Tessa and I walked around with appetizers and then set the platters down on the tables allocated for food.

I waltzed up to the tiki bar and said, "Bartender, give me a drink, would ya?"

Jimmy looked upset. I lost my smile, "Um, did I do something wrong?"

"You mean, other than making my baby girl look like she is seventeen, no, nothing."

"I'm sorry, Jimmy, but Maggie, she's not like me, she's like you, a natural show stopper, and look at her work the crowd. She is amazing."

"I know, that's what I'm afraid of." He ran his hand down his face.

"Well, it's a good thing she has a big, tough daddy, now, isn't it?"

He gazed at me. "Yeah, I'll invest in a few more baseball bats. That's ten for you later, missy."

"What, why?" I asked, giving him my own big doe eyed look.

He laughed. "For making her older, dammit. You're right; she is incredible. She's got it all, and you gave her the one thing she's been lacking."

I looked at him questioningly.

"Confidence, T, you gave her confidence and showed her what she could be, something I could never have done for her in a million years. Thank you."

I batted my eyes. "So, does that mean I get out of my ten?"

"Hell no, you get twenty now. I'm going to stripe that fine ass of yours, and then I'm going to fuck it."

Yikes. I quickly looked around to make sure no one had overheard. Then I strutted away, shaking my ass a bit for him, and headed to the pool to get the games going. At 4:00, Tessa, Al and I carried out the burger bar top that we'd created inside the garage. Jimmy moved from the bar to the barbeque, and Al took over the tiki bar.

The party was a hit, Maggie a star, and I couldn't wait to unleash my last surprise. At 5:30, Tessa, Al, and Jimmy got the kids changed back from swimwear and into their beach wear, then into the house for present opening and cake. I stayed long enough to sing *Happy Birthday* and then snuck out to get the band set up.

Maggie had been begging since yesterday for me to tell her who would be playing. She probably figured it was some local group. But I had gotten her favorite band, J.C. They would play from 6:30 until 8:00. I ran around the pool and straightened out chairs, placing items in baskets and bringing in the empty containers from the burger bar, collecting empty cups, and moving the patio furniture further back from the stage to create a dance floor. Basically, making everything perfect for round two.

The band came through the side, to keep from being spotted by the kids inside. It was dusk, so I turned on the pool lights, the tiki bar lights, the stage lights, and lit the lanterns. The backyard transformed from beach party to something from a resort. When the band was ready, I had them stand behind the stage. Jimmy had hung up a divider to give the band a backdrop for their show.

I came in and nodded to Jimmy; it was perfect timing, because most of the kids were done eating their cake and looking for something to do. We rounded everyone up and headed out to the back. I heard many wows from the kids as they headed over to the stage. I wanted Jimmy to do the introduction part, but he said it was my show and I needed to be the one.

I took the stage and grabbed the microphone. "Thank you, everyone, for coming to Maggie's sweet thirteen. On my thirteenth birthday, her father, Jimmy, my best friend, and his mother had a party for me. I was honored when Maggie asked me to return the favor. She is a most remarkable young woman. I love you, farfallina." I gazed at her as I said it, truly loving the incredible young woman. Instead of being embarrassed, she glowed and sent me a kiss. I grinned and winked. "Now, please put your hands together for J.C."

The look of shock as the band came out from behind the partition was priceless. The lead singer stopped to give Maggie a hug before she took the stage. J.C. band was known for playing dance music, so the minute they started, everyone was grooving, including the adults. The last song they played before they took a break was their most well known, and they invited the birthday girl to come up and perform with them.

Maggie was an incredible dancer, and I think being on that stage with her favorite band was a gift. She grooved and sang backup and was completely amazing. Jimmy and I laughed and sang and clapped and cheered her on, as did all the kids. It was quite a moment.

When the band took their thirty-minute break between sets, they happily hung out with the kids. When they took the stage for their second set, Jimmy dropped the balloons while I fired off pictures. This had turned out better than I could have imagined. The kids were grooving and high fiving each other. They were so thrilled, and glancing at Maggie, she was so happy. I'd done it. I'd pulled it off, and the relief I felt was apparent when I cut loose and danced my heart out with Jimmy.

The last song was *Happy Birthday*, and then it was over. Parents started showing up right after the birthday song ended, and by nine, the band and all the kids were gone, except Emma, who was staying for a sleepover.

Before heading up, Maggie stopped to hug her father and then me. "Thank you, again, Dad, Theresa; this was a birthday dream come true."

"I'm so glad, Maggie. You were incredible. You looked like a movie star. How did it feel to take charge like you did?"

"Funny thing, it was easy, like it came naturally that I would be the leader and the hostess."

"You have your father's best qualities, so I'm not surprised. Happy thirteenth, beautiful."

She hugged me again, and to my surprise, so did Emma. My eyes were a little teary as I watched the girls take off up the stairs.

Jimmy was behind me and wrapped his arms around me.

"Is that what it's like to be a parent, Jimmy? To feel love and to be proud and want the best for them?"

"Yes, T, that is exactly what it's like, and you were awesome, just like a mom would be. Thank you for that, for making her day so special."

"Jimmy Falcone, no need to thank me. You made all of mine special, well, the ones you were there for."

He flinched. "What about the ones I wasn't there for, how did those go?"

"You don't want to know, exactly as expected, I guess. Anyway, I don't want to talk about that. I can't change the past, only look forward to future ones with you and Maggie."

Jimmy handed me a glass of wine, and we sank into the overstuffed chairs in front of the fireplace. I was mentally exhausted from the day but felt good other than that.

"Theresa, do you remember your sixth birthday when the clown came? You were so sure you knew how he did his tricks and you wouldn't stop bugging him until he showed you."

"Yeah." I laughed. "I remember he was kind of creepy. I'm not fond of clowns."

"I remember when you turned three, and my mother baked you a miniature pavlova cake all for you. You wanted to feed me. You kept putting your tiny hand in the cake and then into my mouth. I fell in love with that cute little girl. Al reminded me today how smitten I was with you right from the beginning."

I smiled lethargically. "I wish I remembered her, but I feel—"

Jimmy cut me off. "Don't say broken, Theresa. You're no different than all of us, a little broken. You just need to learn that there is nothing perfect in this world. Well, except maybe your ass."

I laughed, and he joined me. We shared stories for the rest of the evening. When it was time for sleep, I was out in seconds, the long day finally catching up.

Jimmy

I woke early to get a head start on cleaning. I was shocked when Maggie and Emma joined me. They would help if I asked, but volunteering, I'd never seen either of them do that before. The three of us went out back. I picked up and disposed of any remaining garbage, while the girls deflated the penguins and the flamingos. I was close enough to hear their conversation about last night. "Do you think Theresa would do my party?" Em asked Mags.

"I can ask. She's the best, isn't she?'

"Oh yeah, she is and super-hot, too. Did you see the boys checking out her ass?"

"Oh my God, seriously? Well, that's okay, they can ogle all they want, as long as my dad doesn't catch them." They giggled. It was hard not to laugh outright and join in the fun. But I was eavesdropping so kept quietly busy.

"What did you think of Damon? He sure took an interest in you, Mags."

"Oh yeah, he's cute, and he kept his hands to himself. He's cool, for someone our age."

"You mean you don't like him as much as Dean?"

"Dean is like so hot, and he's so popular, I don't stand a chance."

The girls moved along to the other side of the pool, and all I could hear now was the occasional giggle.

When T came downstairs and plunked herself down at the kitchen table, the entire backyard was done. I handed her a peppermint mocha, and she sighed in contentment as she settled into her chair. "Thank you, coffee god," she said with a smile.

Her hair was up in a messy bun, her face devoid of makeup, and she was wearing blue satin loungers that matched her eyes. She looked almost as young as Maggie. I watched her take her first sip, enjoying the contentment that showed on her face as she closed her eyes for a moment and savored the flavor. She was here with me, and sometimes I had to pinch myself. I didn't realize how much I had missed her until she was back in my life.

She took a few more sips and then stood. "I guess I better get a move on. Sorry I slept in. I'm not used to partying with kids."

I was about to answer that it was done and to relax, when the girls came flying around the corner. "Theresa!" they shouted in unison.

She startled, almost spilling her coffee. "Good morning, beauties," she said with a smile.

"Theresa," Em started, "will you organize my birthday party, please, please, please? Mags's party was beyond. It's what all the kids will be talking about come Monday."

Before Theresa could answer, they dragged her outside, coffee in hand. She was unused to so much attention. I would have to help her establish boundaries with her work time and her extracurricular activities. I was about to rescue her, when

Tessa showed up to take the girls to dance, and Al was waiting out front to take me to football.

"Enjoy the silence," I called as I headed to the door, "and be good." *Or not*, I thought. I really liked it when she got into trouble and earned a spanking.

Chapter 13

Jimmy

A l and I were alone in the car; it was as good a time as any to get back to our topic from yesterday. After my initial prodding, the conversation fizzled out, and we were separated for pretty much the remainder of the party. He knew something, but what? I hoped he could shed some light on what, if anything, my dad was up to. "Al, how's your pops doing?"

"Ah, you know, Jimmy, down in Florida with your dad being a bum, go figure, eh. Will that be us when we're their age?"

I laughed. "Probably not. I can't see Maggie taking over the family business."

He laughed and agreed, "Good point."

"Al, what do you know of the old days, you know, when our dads moved from Sicily and my pops started this construction business, which has turned into a monolithic business nightmare for me?"

"Not much, why? Somethin' bugging you?"

I didn't answer his question but asked another of my own, "You met Joe; what do you think of him?"

He concentrated on his driving, and when he answered, I could tell it was right from the heart. "I don't trust the guy."

I sighed. His answer told me two things: one, he wasn't in on any elaborate scheme with Joe, and two, he wasn't party to why Joe was sent. "Do you think my pops sent Joe here to spy on me? Seriously, he knows dick about construction, so why does Pop want me to find a place for him?"

Al concentrated again on the road ahead. "It's not my place to say what or who, but I have wondered that myself. I asked my pops a few days ago when he called to catch up. Your dad is paying off someone in Sicily, someone he was in business with at the beginning when he started here. More than that, Pops wouldn't say. You know Joe has a sister? She is supposed to be a knockout and the brain in the family. Joe invited her to Philly and used his new expense account you gave him to take her out on the town, expensive dinners and clubs. Did you know?"

I was shocked; I had no idea. "I know less than you, my friend, but tomorrow I will get to the bottom of it. He's not draining my company. I don't give a shit what deal my father made twenty-five years ago, surely cash will make this asshole go away."

We arrived at the field. The rest of the guys were warming up. I was happy to see that Josh had accepted my invitation to join us while Bobby worked on staging a few condos for me. "Al," I grabbed his arm before we exited his vehicle, "don't say nothin' to no one, capiche? And thanks, friend, for having my back."

"Anything, Jimmy, you know that."

Theresa

A day alone in the ginormous house felt weird. I spent some time setting up my things in my office space that Jimmy had allocated for my use. I sat down afterward and did some work. I uploaded the photos from Maggie's party and wrote a new blog entry on my first experience as a party planner. I didn't include photos of anyone, not even myself, just of the set up and the food. The theme was *Keeping Up With the Kids, the Impact on the Mind and Body*.

The private photos I uploaded into a shared cloud account that Maggie could access and use what she wanted for her social media accounts. I took a break after that and went for a swim in the pool, using the water as my workout partner instead of the track.

I stepped out of the pool an hour later and went for a sauna and a shower. Jimmy had some wonderful extras in his home that I was only beginning to enjoy. An hour later, I headed to the kitchen to make some lunch. Too hungry to cook, I warmed up some leftovers instead. I received a text from Jimmy and was about to text him back when I heard the security system beep that it was deactivated.

I glanced up at the monitor. Someone was entering though the garage door into the main foyer.

> *(me) Someone's here, what do I do?*
> *(Jimmy) What? Hide. I'm on my way and Josh is*
> *with me.*

I quickly turned the phone to mute and looked for a hiding spot. I spotted the back staircase to the upper level. I moved fast, as I heard shoes moving across the tiled floor in the great room. Whoever it was, they were close. My blood froze in my veins. What was going on? This wasn't a break in, whoever was in the house assumed no one was home, and they were in no rush.

Thank God the stairs were carpeted. I went into Maggie's room; she had a safety room in there that was completely hidden. I got in and closed the door behind me, just as I heard steps coming down the hallway. I knew it was soundproof, but I put a hand over my mouth anyway. I could see through the camera that whoever it was had stopped in Maggie's room and was looking around. I could only see them from the knees down as they were too close. But when the person turned to close the door, I saw his face—it was Joe.

That piece of shit, what did he think he was doing? Did he know I was here alone, was that his plan? I got up and out of my hiding spot. I wanted to follow him and see where he went. I didn't think my life was in danger, but who knew. I slowly opened the second door in the closet and stepped out.

Peering around the corner and down the hall, I was in time to see him disappear into Jimmy's room. I heard drawers opening and closing. Okay, so he was looking for something. I poked my head in just as a text came in from Jimmy, who was smart enough not to run in and yell for me. *Don't make any noise, he's in your room right now going through your drawers. Meet me at the back stairs*, I replied.

I tiptoed back down the hall and down the back stairs, meeting Jimmy and Josh in the great room. I threw myself into Jimmy's arms, needing his temporary embrace.

"He's upstairs rummaging through your room; it's Joe."

Jimmy

I felt the blood in my veins freeze. What the hell was going on? I decided not to call him out, instead, we went into the security room and watched what was going on. He was looking for something, and then the bastard found it, the button to the hidden safe that slowly lifted and came from the depths of my nightstand drawer. There was no money in that safe, only documents.

He still needed the code to open the safe. I watched him, and he knew my old code, which meant someone gave it to him, and the only person who knew it was my pops. I changed it when Theresa moved in and never told him. It didn't seem important with him in Florida; he wouldn't be doing any business down there. Or would he? Maybe the man I'd known and emulated my entire life was a lie. I had questions, and Joe was going to answer them. I had him on video footage. Theresa was a witness and I could have him arrested.

We watched him give up in frustration and leave the room. We followed him on the monitor as he came back down the stairs and through the great room. I nodded to Josh, and we stepped out of the security room.

Josh yelled, "Stop, you're under arrest."

Joe took off like a shot, but my much longer legs caught up to him and I tackled him to the ground. Josh slapped some handcuffs on him, and we sat him down on a chair in the middle of the room. I felt like I was in a gangster movie.

I was sweating and wondering how this would all play out. Josh was cool, showing absolutely no emotion. I decided to copy him and created a blank look as I sat down in a chair opposite Joe. Josh remained standing, with his gun pointed at Joe.

"This is how this is going to play out, Joe. You can either talk to me here and I won't press charges, or we can take you down to the station. I have you on video, and I also have a witness."

He sneered at me like I was less than gum on the bottom of his shoe. "Go ahead, Falcone. If you arrest me,

I will be out in an hour. We Marenos have a long reach, straight to the local cops. We have people in every city eating out of our hands, so if you think one little copper is going to scare me, you got another thing coming, Jimmy."

I decided to ignore his remarks for now. "You wanted in my personal safe. There is nothing in there but documents, why?"

He said nothing, just sat there with a smug look on his face that I wanted to erase with my fist.

"If this is about money, I am more than happy to pay off any debt my father created with yours."

His expression changed to surprise for a moment; he expected me to be dumb. I was glad I'd broached work with Al this morning. "That's why you're here, right, to collect on a debt; give me a number."

He sneered again, "You're so stupid, Falcone, you think this is just about money? It's a blood debt, to be paid with many assets, including your sweet little Theresa."

I punched him in the face, I couldn't hold back anymore. "Jimmy, stand down," Josh demanded.

"That's right, Jimmy, be a good boy and do what everyone tells you to do." He kissed the air and blew it at me. Asshole. "I have nothing else to say; arrest me."

Josh radioed in for backup. I disappeared back into the security room where I'd told Theresa to stay hidden. I phoned Al. "Yeah, everything's okay. I need to talk to you. Can you get Frank to come with you and bring my car? We have things to discuss." I hung up and gave Theresa a hug. "Stay here until the cops take him away, okay, bella? I will fill you in when he's gone."

She nodded her head and sat down, while I went back out to join Josh and wait for backup. Two minutes later, a cop car came screeching up my driveway. Josh hauled Joe outside and gave the other two a rundown on what had happened. They left for the police station.

"Jimmy, I will call you if we get anything else out of him, but I fear he is right; he will make bail unless he has a record in America, and he'll be free. I don't like what he said. Be careful, step up security and keep Theresa safe. I will look into his family and the connection between him and your family and see if I can find anything out."

"Thanks, Josh." I shook his hand and he left. I retrieved Theresa from the security room and went to the kitchen to make coffee. "We need to talk. Al will be here any minute. You two, I am trusting, nothing goes beyond us, not even with Maggie, understand?"

She nodded and took the coffee I offered her. Al came in and joined us. "Boss, Frank left your car in the driveway; here are the keys." He handed over my keys. "What happened, what's going on?" I filled Theresa in on my conversation in the car with Al, then I filled Al in on what Teresa had speculated about in the restaurant, about my pops and Joe.

Then Theresa shared what she had seen, which I knew already from the security system. "Jimmy, he assumed no one was here; he knows your schedule."

"Yes, and if you hadn't been here, T, it would not have dawned on me to check security footage, as he didn't break in, he had the codes. Al, I need to ramp up my security. New codes, extra curbside patrolling, that kind of thing. I will phone the company and let them know I need to change everything. We need Joe extracted from the company and any funds he has access to denied. If he wants to stay in Philadelphia, he won't be doing it on our dime."

"Did you get any information out of him, boss?"

"Only that he said this was a blood debt to be paid with more than money, whatever the hell that means. He spoke gangster, and despite my place of birth, I am anything but.

What I'm concerned about is him knowing what was in that safe."

"May I ask," Theresa hesitated, "what is in that safe, Jimmy?"

"The deeds to everything. He wanted to take everything. Josh will call if he learns anything, but he thinks Joe will make bail and be out today, so we need to get on this. Al, you have your marching orders. I have calls to make. T, Tessa is bringing Mags home, can you present a united front for me and you two have some girl time? If she sees me, she's going to know something's up; my kid is very perceptive."

"Of course, Jimmy, anything else?"

"Yeah, don't go anywhere, and if you need to, tell me. I'll go with you."

She consented and the three of us moved to our separate tasks. "Not a word to anyone, until we know what's going on. Assume the worst."

Al took his leave and I went to my office—time to call Pops.

"Pops, it's Jimmy, you alone?"

"Jimmy, let me call you back."

I hung up the phone. I was pissed. What the hell had he done? He needed to tell me everything, so I could fix this.

"Jimmy, it's me."

I didn't recognize the number; he must have used a burner phone. "Pops, what in hell is going on? I just had Joe Mareno sneak into our house and try to get into my private safe. What did you do? He said you owe him a blood debt; what the hell does that mean?"

He was quiet for a moment, gathering his thoughts? Or his guts to tell me the truth?

"Jimmy, back before I left Sicily, I ran into some trouble, and Joseph Mareno helped me out. Our deal was a set sum of money, to be paid back by a certain date. I paid him back on time, but if left me penniless. When we arrived in the United States, I had about a hundred dollars in my pocket, and your ma wasn't well. The stress and poverty we'd been living under had taken its toll on her. We have a big family, but no one was doing well financially. That is why so much of our family resides here in the states, instead of Italy. Until the last seven or eight years, we were the only ones who had done well, and I have helped all your cousins get started in business or school here."

He paused for a moment. "But back then, I didn't have anyone. I started working in construction and it got us by, but I wasn't making enough to save and start my business. I called Joseph and asked for another loan. Jimmy, he is old school, cosa nostra. I knew it but thought if I paid him back, our dealings would be finished. But about twelve years ago, long after I'd paid him, he wanted to strike another bargain and I said no. I didn't want anything to do with drug running or guns or anything else. We have a legitimate business that has done unprecedently well, and I want to keep it that way."

He paused again, taking a drink of something, and then continued. "About the same time, we had a visitor at the old place. It was a messenger from Mareno, and he said if I didn't allow his business to use us as a legitimate cover, then he would go after us. I offered him a ridiculous amount of money, Jimmy, but with Mareno, it was personal, because no one says no to the cosa nostra, no matter where you live."

"Pops, he mentioned Theresa, why? And, why did you have us move from the old neighborhood when you did? Does this have something to do with her?"

He sighed, "In a roundabout way, it does. I never meant to put Theresa in danger, Jimmy. But Mareno said the only way to fix this was by connecting our families. Theresa, she was in the way; you were supposed to marry Mareno's daughter, Felicia, join our houses and our business, and run it jointly with Joe."

I couldn't believe what I was hearing. Was he insane? I wasn't marrying anyone but Theresa. I had a sinking feeling that the Marenos were behind everything that had happened. "Pops, was Christina's accident really an accident, or was it a hit?"

"Mareno was afraid that you and Christina would get together because you shared the bond of a child, so he put out the hit on her."

I thought I was going to puke. This was insanity. "And you moved us to get me away from Theresa?"

"I did," he answered quietly.

"Joe breaking in, having the security passcodes, was that you?"

"Yes."

"Pops, why, what were you thinking?"

"Honestly, Jimmy, I don't know what I was thinking, except, I know you have amassed quite a bank account. Both of us could retire if we wanted to. I guess I thought if they broke in and took the deeds, then you would be off the hook for the marriage and the blood debt."

It wasn't a bad plan, but still, there were no guarantees. I needed to think and come up with a plan of my own. "Pops, is there a hit on Theresa?"

Silence answered me. Seconds passed, and when he spoke, his voice was so low I could hardly hear him. "I don't know for sure, but I would assume they would want her removed. Whatever you do, son, be careful."

"You, too, Pops." I hung up the phone and ran my hands through my hair. My first reaction was to run away with Maggie and Theresa. But that wasn't the answer. I needed something iron clad. If I could catch them or prove their illegal dealings, then I could make a deal to bail them out and my company, if need be. I could always start again if I wanted.

I called Josh. "I have an idea I want to run by you. Can we meet?"

"Sure, I was on my way to meet Bobby. He's done with the staging, maybe check it out, and we can talk off record at the same time."

"Perfect." I got on the phone with security and got two teams to watch my place and then went through the process of changing out all the codes.

I was heading out the door when Mags got home. "Where are you going, Daddy?" She pouted.

"Have a meeting, sweets. Theresa is waiting for you; she has some girl stuff planned."

She clapped and squealed and ran off in search of T. I smiled; those two were becoming very close. I had to make sure that whatever I did, it worked, so I could keep my family safe.

Chapter 14

Theresa

Jimmy looked like a man on a mission, his face serious and filled with conflict. I knew he would be okay, but if this was about me, then I wanted to know.

Tessa was about to head home, but I stopped her. "Tessa, do you know what's going on with the company?"

She seemed like she wanted to talk, but in the end, all she said was, "No, I'm sorry, Theresa." Despite my promise to Jimmy, I'd overheard the conversation with Joe while he was tied up. I had turned up the volume while I was hiding in the monitor room and turned it down when Jimmy came back.

I told Maggie we would have a spa evening with take out, but I needed to do a couple of things first. I went into Jimmy's office while he was gone and looked for his father's phone number. James senior was the key to the mystery. Flipping on Jimmy's laptop, I found all the contact information with everyone pertaining to the company. I added James's number to my cell and then turned off the computer. At least now I had it, if I decided to call.

I headed upstairs to get Maggie. We grabbed everything we could possibly need for an at home mani/pedi. Hours later, Jimmy found us sipping health shakes with cucumbers on our eyes. "You're home early. We were going to get take out, any ideas?" I asked.

"No worries, ladies, meet me downstairs in forty-five. I will have dinner ready." He left and we continued our girl chatter. "Maggie, you have the best dad in the world, you know that?"

"Yeah, I'm pretty lucky. He used to worry, I think, you know, that I didn't have a mom. But really, I had Nonna here for me all the time, and Dad, well, he's always been really good at quality time."

I sighed, "Yes, making someone feel special is definitely one of his super powers."

She giggled. "Do you love him, T?"

"More than that, Maggie, I'm crazy in love with him. I think I always have been. Do you feel like that about anyone?"

She thought about it. "Well, I don't know that I'm crazy in love, but there is a boy, Dean, and he is super-hot and super nice. I really like him, but he is two grades ahead of me. I don't think he knows I'm alive."

"Is he on your Instagram?"

"Yes."

"And have you posted your birthday yet?"

"No, Emma posted a few, but mostly of close ups of her with me and our other friends."

"I have an idea; grab your phone."

I grabbed her phone and quickly made a highlight page of her birthday, focusing on her, and then I added sayings on the photos and sent her three separate multi images for her to post. I added the hashtags and a line that said *stay tuned for our next party presented by MagT Entertainment.*

I posted them, and she grabbed her phone from me to see what I'd done. "MagT, that's us," she said excitedly.

"That's right, and if that guy has any brains, he'll be commenting and asking when the next party is. But, if he doesn't, then he isn't the one, Mags. You'll know when you have the one. You will feel tingly and safe and cherished. That's what your dad does for me." We giggled and, setting aside our gadgets, headed downstairs for dinner.

Jimmy

I met up with Josh and Bobby at the renovated complex I'd hired Bobby to stage. I looked in on the three suites he'd done and was blown away. "Bobby, this is amazing; you have a gift, man."

He looked pleased.

"Damn it, Jimmy, don't give him a big head. He's hard to live with as it is," Josh said with a smirk on his face.

Bobby returned this with, "Oh, please, boyfriend, you are so jealous."

I laughed at their antics. "Josh, anything from Joe yet?"

He shook his head. "But we still have him for a few hours. He doesn't have a record in the United States, but he has been arrested several times in Italy and does hold a record there. Apparently, he did some nasties for the newly dead crime boss, Salvatore Riina. I'm looking for any connection between Mareno and your father, Jimmy, but so far, nothing."

"You won't find one. I spoke with my father. He got a straight up loan from Joe's dad, Joseph Mareno Sr., thirty years ago, in Sicily, then again when he moved to America, about twenty-five years ago. My father paid them back, but with the success of our company here, Mareno wants to use it to hide illegal dealings between the U.S. and Europe. According to my father, the only way out of this mess is if I marry Mareno's only daughter and share my company fifty-fifty with Joe. Then what they call a blood debt will be repaid. They mean business. I found out from my pops that Mareno ordered the hit on Maggie's mother; it wasn't an accident."

"You won't do it, of course, you won't break Theresa's heart again, will you?" Bobby asked.

"No, I won't, but I may make it look like I am. There is a hit out on Theresa. If I don't do something, the cosa nostra will take out everyone I love, even Maggie, if I don't bend. Pretending to cut her loose in a public location could be the only thing that protects her while I work on a way out of this."

Bobby digested this information, and his eyes lit up. "Wait, Josh, if the Mareno family is responsible for getting Maggie's mother killed, maybe if you looked up the report and could prove it, then you would have a reason to try to convict Joe, or… get him to back off and go free; you know, that detective FBI thing you do so well."

Josh replied, "It isn't that easy, Bobby, but getting it moved from accident to murder could certainly help. I'll see what I can dig up."

"Be careful, Josh, you heard Joe today; they have cops on the payroll all over the U.S."

"What are you going to do, Jimmy? I can help with protection if you want. I have some friends, retired cops and ex-military, who run a security firm. Want me to put you in touch?"

I nodded. "Yes, that would be good. I don't want anything happening to my girls. And, Bobby, if something goes wrong and you see me dumping T, you know it's a ruse. Don't believe it, and I will only do it as a last straw, you understand?"

"I do. I just hope she does."

"Me, too, Bobby, and I'm counting on you to help me if this goes south."

He nodded. We said our goodbyes and I set off to see my lawyer. It was a Sunday, but he was willing to meet with me.

Jon Gigliotti was a partner in one of the top law firms in all of Philadelphia and a long-time friend of the family.

I quickly gave him a basic rundown without getting into much detail, but enough to show him I was in dire need of shifting the company. "Jon, I was thinking, could I sell the company to Joe Mareno for one dollar? But without the non-competition clause. I want to be able to start again, from scratch, with no interference. If they get what they want, then maybe they will back off."

Jon sat back in his chair and thought. "The problem I see, Jimmy, is these gentlemen don't seem to honor payment. Your father has already gone down this road and yet, as soon as the company did better than anyone could have predicted, he wanted more, and isn't that what the cosa nostra do? They have a code, but they are greedy. If you did this, and Joe ran your old company into the ground, or it was dissolved because of its illegal activities, they would come looking for you again, and what's to stop history from repeating itself?"

"Good call; I never even thought of that. So, what do you think I should do?"

"A few ideas: either leave this type of business behind and move to a state where there is very little mafia. Or, start a new business, have it be owned by a dummy company so it can't be attained by outside forces. Or, make yourself a nice little ma and pa business that doesn't net more than 100k per year, so you're under their radar. Lastly, if somehow you could catch them in a crime, then you could do your idea, offer them the sale of your company for a dollar and hold over their head the crime that you will go to the FBI with."

My mind was racing. "Thanks, Jon, and if I need you to draw up documents in a hurry, you'll be available?"

He said "of course" as he shook my hand.

I drove home and found my ladies with cucumbers on their eyes, laughing like they were best friends. I smiled at the two of them and prayed I wouldn't have to cut Theresa loose, but I did know that if I couldn't protect her, then that was exactly what I would have to do.

After dinner, Maggie scooted upstairs to get her homework done before bed. I threw Theresa over my shoulder like a Neanderthal and headed for our room. She was still owed a spanking and an ass fucking. "Strip," I demanded as I deposited her on the bed.

She stripped and placed some pillows at the end of the bed, hiking her perfect ass in the air. I felt my cock harden; seeing those creamy mounds created a desire to fuck her until she screamed. "All right, little girl, why are we here?"

"Um, I, uh, don't remember," she answered honestly.

It was hard not to laugh. Here she was, surrendering her ass for punishment, and she had no idea why, but still, she gave herself to me. I stood behind her, rubbing her ass. She moaned and arched up in my hands.

"Twenty, bella, ten because I said so, and ten more… because I said so." She smiled while she moaned. My woman was so sweet, so perfect, how I loved her. I decided to give her twenty with my hand and see how she did with that. If she was still panting like a wanton, I would give her more before I took her.

I used medium force when I brought my hand down repeatedly and quickly in succession, reaching twenty in mere seconds. I stopped and rubbed. Her slit was glistening; she was super turned on. I ran a finger along the seam of her pussy all the way to her little back button. She squirmed and arched, wanting my cock.

I peppered her ass slowly, with twenty more well placed smacks to her sit spots, warming up her ass for my cock. She was ready for me. Pushing the pillows out of the way, I pressed her chest farther down into the bed as I pulled her by the hips to the edge. I lubed her ass with her own juices and pressed one finger inside. She mewled like a kitten. I rained down smacks on her backside with my other hand while she gyrated against my finger.

I stopped spanking and removed my finger, replacing it with my cock. She tightened as I slid the head of my cock inside her ass. I stopped, allowing her to catch her breath and relax her muscles. I reached under and played with her labia and then inserted three fingers into her dripping pussy.

"Jimmy, oh, yes, more, please, more."

I pressed my hard cock all the way into her ass and held still while I continued to work my fingers in and out of her pussy. She began to move along my shaft, causing the most delicious friction. "That's right, baby, fuck my cock, take it the way you like it."

She fucked my cock like a champion while I continued to plunge my fingers in and out. "Jimmy, Sir, please may I come?"

"Come, Theresa." I felt her muscles convulse around my fingers and my cock. She was tight and felt amazing. "Again, Theresa, do it again," I said as I pinched her clit. She yelled out her second release, shuddering as she came down. I plunged my fingers into her, and she and I came simultaneously. I filled her ass while her juices dripped down my fingers. I needed the release, and I know she did. I pulled out and then drew her to her feet. "Let's shower, Tesoro, I want to clean you."

As we lay in bed afterward, cuddling, Theresa asked me, "Jimmy, are there any updates? Was I right about Christina?"

"You were, T. It was a hit, by Joe's family. As to who exactly did it, we don't know, but Josh is looking into it."

She was quiet for a moment, then asked, "Is there a hit on me?"

I didn't want to tell her. I wanted to lie, but I was pretty sure she would know. "Yes, Theresa, that is why you must be careful. Tell me or your new security detail where you are at all times, and make sure you always have protection with you."

She didn't respond. "Theresa," I growled. "I'm serious. I will shred your ass if you do anything stupid, do you hear me?"

"Yes." She sighed. "I hear you. I was talking to Tessa today. I asked her about Christina. She said I look a lot like her, and I was wondering, if, well, like me, did you have a type? Did the women you dated or had sex with remind you of me?"

"What difference does it make, T? We're together now."

She sat up, facing me, her face angry. "Because, Jimmy, don't you get it? Maggie and I look alike. I could be her mother or older sister. You must have had a type, just answer my damn question."

"First of all, don't demand. I am looking for your motivation in asking, and why did you talk to Tessa about Christina? What did you want to know?"

"I didn't ask about her looks. I only asked if she had met her, and she said only once. She said that all your one-night stands looked alike, that she couldn't keep track and that they all looked a little like me. It made me feel better to know I wasn't the only idiot trying to find what I had with you with other men."

I pulled her back down and into my arms. "Yes, T, every girl had something you had, either the eyes or the hair color or a mannerism. I looked for you in every girl I spent time with. Does that make you feel better?"

She blew her bangs off her forehead, her attempt at looking annoyed. "Yes."

"Yes, what?" I asked. She didn't answer. I began to tickle her. "Yes, what?"

"Yes, oh God, please stop, yes, Sir."

"Good girl," I soothed, kissing her neck. "Now, let's go to sleep. I have to head in early to work tomorrow."

"Do you want me to take Maggie to school?"

"No, T, I'd rather you stay here. I will take Maggie to school."

She hesitated. "You're not going to make me a princess imprisoned in the tower, here, are you?"

"And if I am, what are you going to do about it? What if I decided to tie you to my bed for a month and only untie you to let you pee and bathe?"

She laughed. "Then I guess I'd say, as long as I get spanked and fucked every day, I'm okay with that."

I laughed. "Tesoro, you make me happy, you know that?"

She sighed as she snuggled back as far into me as she could. "Yes, Jimmy, I know that, and you make me happy, too." She sighed again and then stilled, already asleep.

Chapter 15

Theresa

I knew Jimmy was working on a plan. The fact he was no longer sharing what he knew with me meant that, somehow, I was involved.

After Jimmy and Maggie left that morning, I phoned his father. "Hello, Mr. Falcone, this is Theresa Romano."

Dead silence from the other end.

"I know you don't want to speak with me, but I need to know one thing. Is Jimmy in danger because of me?"

Again, silence. I prayed the answer was no, that this was just a giant mistake.

"Theresa, in a roundabout way, yes, but that's all I can say. If you want to know more, you must talk to Jimmy, himself. I wish things had been different; I know how much my son loves you, but hear me, Theresa, he has been slated in for something else, something beyond my control or his. If you stay, you will only make things harder."

"Thank you for your honesty," I said and hung up the phone. I knew in my gut, even back when we were kids, that

James was against us being a match, and he had probably moved the family when he saw the inevitability of us being together in the future. I loved Jimmy and Maggie, but if staying endangered him, them, then I needed to leave.

I decided to call Bobby and see if he would talk me out of it. "Hey, T, what's up?"

"Bobby, do you know what's going on? Has Josh told you anything?"

A slight hesitation, followed by, "Not really, why?"

"I spoke with Jimmy's father, and he told me that my being here is endangering Jimmy, and I'm thinking I need to go. What do you think I should do?"

"T, listen, girl, you need to talk to him. I'm sure he has a plan, and you taking off might put his plan in jeopardy. Maybe leaving, at least for a little while, is a good thing, but I don't know. I can't answer that for you."

"Okay." I sighed. "Later," and I pressed end on my cell.

I texted Josh.

(Me) Need to talk, can you come by?

I didn't trust that my phone hadn't been tampered with. I needed Josh to run a scan on my number and let me know who, if anyone, was listening in and how traceable I was.

(Josh) Yep, see you shortly. Don't answer until you know it's me, Theresa.
(Me) okay

His extra warning spoke volumes; something big was happening in the Falcone world. When Josh arrived, he texted me that he was out front. I double checked the security footage and then let him in. I felt like I was living in Fort

Knox, and I didn't like it one bit. I ushered him in, and we went to the kitchen for coffee.

"Josh, I need some help, but first of all, do you know what's happening with Jimmy and Joe?"

"Only some, Theresa, but I can't share anything with you at this point."

"Damn, no one wants to answer me. At least Jimmy's father gave me some honesty."

Josh's eyes perked up at the mention of the elder Falcone. "What exactly did he say?"

I shared with him my conversation with James. "And he thinks I'm endangering Jimmy by being here. I need to know if you agree," I finished.

He pursed his lips, considering his answer. "I don't know. I agree with Bobby—he texted me after you called him—you should talk to Jimmy. He's a smart guy, Theresa. If he can find an honest way out of this shit, he'll do it. Then again, he might not get the chance; the odds are stacked against him."

Maybe with me out of the game, he would think more clearly. "I know what I need to do, and I need your help." I shared my plan with him, and he agreed to help me.

Jimmy

I decided to rip off the Band-Aid and call a meeting with the big guns. Joseph would fly out from Italy and arrive in the states the day after tomorrow. I had a few days to get my plan in place. That night at dinner, the energy was subdued, all except Maggie. She was as bubbly as ever and talked Theresa's ear off about an Instagram post T had done for her.

"Maggie, I told you no social media. How do you know

T's posts were a hit if you're not on there?" I thought I'd caught her in a lie.

"Oh, Daddy, because, at school today, all anyone was talking about was the party created by MagT Entertainment." She giggled. "Seriously, like it's totally trending right now, Dad."

Theresa smiled. "I'm glad for you, Maggie, and Dean, did he say anything?"

"Yes!" she shouted. "He came up to my locker and said he hopes he gets an invite to my next party and he winked. Seriously, T! At me! Then he said he'd see me later and headed off for class. I almost turned into a puddle right there on the floor."

Theresa and Maggie both started laughing and then they did some high five combination, and I shook my head. In a few short weeks, my daughter and my girlfriend had become besties. "Do I want to know who this Dean fellow is or what you two are talking about?"

They both turned and said, "No," at the same time and then went into more peals of laughter.

I shook my head again, amused. "I really like seeing you two together having fun; it warms my heart." It was meant to be an 'aw' moment, and it was for Maggie, but Theresa had a flash of an emotion I didn't want to see. Defeat.

I questioned her about it later, and of course, I had to spank it out of her. She fought but not really. I think she liked to put on a show of resistance so I wouldn't know how much pleasure she really derived from being spanked. Of course, I knew; it was my job to know.

"Ouch, Jimmy, stop, please."

"Only if you start talking, Tesoro. What's going on with you, and if you tell me nothing again, I will go in to the bathroom and get the wooden bath brush. You know how much you hate that, so spill, already."

I was holding her over my lap, with one leg over hers, her perfect ass red with my handprints. I wanted to fuck her and bring her pleasure, but I needed answers first. "I just wish you would tell me what's going on, Jimmy. It appears you either don't want to or can't; either way, it makes me sad."

I pulled her up to my lap and took her chin in my hand. "Listen, T, there are things I can't tell you yet, because I'm still formulating my moves. No one knows my plan, but a few know the pieces I need them to know. I can't risk telling you, in case something happens to you. The less you know, the better. I know this is hard, but I need you to trust me."

She sighed and gazed into my eyes. "I do trust you, Jimmy, that's never in question, nor is my love for you. But I get the feeling that I am in the way. Joe said it, that I was part of it; I heard him on the monitor."

So, that's what this was about. I put some steel in my eyes and said, "So you think it's okay to disobey me?" I flung her back down and over my lap, smacking away with double the intensity.

"I didn't," she yelped. "I never left the room, only turned up the volume."

Damn, the girl was clever. I sat her back up, and she winced when her backside was firmly on my lap. "You're right, you didn't disobey. I will tell you one thing I found out, because you being in the know won't change anything or put you in harm's way."

She looked eager for what I was about to share. I wish she didn't, because it wasn't pleasant. "There is a deal. I won't tell you more about that piece, my marriageable status, blood debt as the Mareno family is calling it, involves me marrying his only daughter. That's why Joe mentioned you; for me to marry his sister, you would need to be out of the picture."

I don't know what she was expecting, but it wasn't that. She paled and then swallowed. "I see."

"No, Theresa, I don't think you do. I am not marrying anyone but you. I don't care what they want. The head of the family, Joseph Mareno, is flying out from Italy. I am meeting him on Wednesday. I have a lot to put in place before then—information that I need confirmed—before I proceed. Don't worry. I would walk from the business, and Philadelphia, if it came to that."

What I said should have reassured her. No matter what, I chose her. But she didn't seem at peace at all. I moved her off my lap and onto the bed. I would fuck all thought from her head and then see how she was in the morning.

***

Theresa

Jimmy moved me to the bed and spread my legs. Of course, I was soaked. I always was when he spanked me, but my mind was somewhere else, already embarking on the plan I'd set in motion with Josh.

My body was all Jimmy's, however, and when he ran his tongue from my clit to my anus, I arched toward his mouth ready for more, ready to be ravaged. This could be the last time, for a while, or forever. That remained to be seen.

He soaked my back hole with his tongue and then pressed his thumb inside me. I moaned in pleasure. He worked a finger inside my other hole, and I bucked my hips against both fingers. I wanted him to go deep, so deep that all thought and emotion would be gone. I wanted to be nothing more than a wanton, mewling mess of a human, begging for his touch, for the release I craved.

He flipped me onto my tummy and pulled me to the edge of the bed. He lifted my lower half off the bed so all that anchored me to the earth was my hands. Then he plunged his face between my thighs, sending shocking ripples through my sex. I gushed, and he moaned as he licked. Then he lowered me and changed arm position.

He wrapped his strong forearms around my thighs and spread me wide as he lifted my pelvis into the air. He slammed his cock into me in one thrust, and I screamed at the intensity of it. "Oh, my fucking God, Jimmy, fuck, yes, holy shit, it's so fucking *intense!*" I screamed the last word, and my world spilled as multiple orgasms ripped through my body.

"Theresa," he barked as he came hard. He gently let me down. Both of us were quivering with the intensity of the release; it was all he could do to climb on the bed. We lay there, cuddling and panting in the aftermath. I woke sometime later to the sound of the shower then again, when he wiped me and put me to bed.

I slept like the dead until dawn's first light came peeking through the blinds. I got up and raced quietly to my office. I sent Josh a message, then I crept back to bed. My plan was in place and would be rolling out later in the day.

After Maggie and Jimmy left, I grabbed my laptop, chargers, makeup, and clothing essentials and threw everything into one duffle bag, all I had left of my dad's stuff. I waited for Josh, and while I did, I wrote a note to Jimmy.

I love you, Jimmy Falcone, more than my own life. I am going into hiding so you are free to do what you need to. Please be safe, Theresa

I put it on his office desk, in front of the picture of the three of us on our big night out. Josh texted and told me to go out the back door and down the side of the house, skip over the hedge at the back neighbors'; they weren't home and didn't have security. He'd checked, and he said to meet him on the next street.

I threw on my baseball cap and sunglasses, and with duffle in hand, followed his instructions. I jumped in his car. He took off, and it took me a minute to realize that the man driving wasn't Josh, it was Joe!

I knew my text messages had Josh on the top, and I managed to get off one message, *HELP,* before the goon who'd been hiding in the back got it from me. I wrestled for it, but Joe managed to knock me out while I was busy wrestling with back seat goon.

When I woke, I was in a warehouse. I kept my head down to appear asleep. It was a Falcone warehouse; what the hell was going on? They should have been thrilled I left Jimmy, so he could marry Joe's sister.

I tried moving, but my ankles and wrists were tied. I looked around. There were only a few people in the warehouse. I didn't recognize anyone, that is, not until Al's car pulled in. I was elated and was about to shout out to him when he stepped out of his car, but he didn't seem surprised to see me tied up on the floor. He went and shook hands with Joe. That bastard, Jimmy's best friend had turned on him. Maybe there was a reasonable explanation; maybe they had something over his head as well.

He spoke with Joe and then headed back to his car and left the warehouse. Damn, now what? I saw shoes walking toward me. Joe tugged my chin upward. "Nice shiner, Theresa," he sneered, "it will go far in driving Jimmy insane."

He hauled me to my feet. "In fact, a little more bruising should have him begging at our feet." He slapped me, hard, several times. I felt blood in my mouth and knew my lip was split. I felt fear welling up and I started to panic. Joe was short but built like a bull; he hefted me up onto his shoulder easily and walked to a van, where he threw me inside and locked the doors.

Jimmy

I had been texting Josh all morning but had heard nothing back. I finally gave in and phoned Bobby.

"Hey, where is Josh? We were supposed to meet this morning."

"Jimmy, I am at the hospital with Josh. He was shot, but the bullet only grazed him. He's going to be okay. Wait, he wants to talk to you."

"Jimmy, listen, Theresa is in danger. I think Joe may have her."

I felt the blood drain from my face. "How do you know?" I asked, hearing the hollowness in my voice.

"She was going to leave today. I was helping her, but I was shot from behind and then knocked unconscious and left in an alley two blocks from your house. I don't know who else it could have been."

Joe was an animal. I shuddered to think what he would do with her. "I need to go and get her, Josh."

"No, Jimmy, listen, you need to come to my place. Bobby and I will be leaving the hospital in a few minutes. I have more to tell you. But I wanted to warn you, in case you get messages from the Mareno family. They won't harm Theresa, at least not yet. They will want to use her to force you into accepting their plan, but we still have a card to play, so don't let anything you see or hear put her at risk. Come to my place. I promise you, we will get her back."

I hung up the phone with Josh and called my pops.

"Jimmy, how are you?"

"They have Theresa, Pops. I have to save her."

"Jimmy, listen to me, don't do anything rash. Just give them what they want, and they will let Theresa go."

My eyes widened in shock. "You knew," I accused.

He was silent. "Why, Pops, why not tell me?"

"I tried telling you, Jimmy, they want a blood debt, and I told Theresa she was in the way, that if she loved you, she would leave. I guess they decided to make sure that she was out of the way. Just be thankful she isn't dead."

I hung up. My own father! What next? Then an image of Al entered my mind. No, not Al, but I had to be sure. I texted my daughter, *don't go anywhere with Emma and Tessa today, Maggie. Go anywhere you want, but be with other kids, and no matter what, do not go into Al or Tessa's car, promise me.*

She texted me immediately.

> *(Maggie) Daddy, are you okay? You're scaring me.*
> *(Me) I will explain it all later, Mags, but I need you to go somewhere safe. Are you near this Dean kid?*
> *(Maggie) Yes, Daddy.*
> *(Me) Give him the phone.*
> *(Maggie) Yes, Daddy.*

I stopped texting and called my daughter's cell. A young man with a strong voice answered.

"Dean?"

"Yes, sir?"

"Are you a reliable kid?" I asked.

"Yes, sir," he replied.

"What's your last name?"

"DeLuca, sir."

"I need you to do me a favor, Dean Deluca. Take my daughter to your place after school and don't let her go anywhere with anyone else. Do you understand?"

"Yes, sir."

"Good. Mags will give you my number. Text me when you get there and I will text you when I'm on my way. Thank you, Dean."

"No problem, sir."

I hung up and raced over to Bobby and Josh's on the other side of town. They buzzed me in, and I flew up the stairs to their unit.

Bobby answered the door and gave me a hug. "Come on in, Jimmy. Drink?"

I shook my head; alcohol would dull my senses, and I was already high on adrenalin. Coffee would make me snap. Josh was resting on the couch. He made to stand when he saw me, and I waved him down. "Don't move, Josh. Now tell me what the hell is going on."

Bobby and Josh both started babbling at the same time about Theresa, but different stories.

"Stop." I held up my hand. "Bobby, you first."

He filled me in on his phone call with Theresa and then said he'd told Josh.

Josh then took over and explained his meeting at the house with her yesterday and their game plan. It would have been good, had it worked out, Josh said. "She texted me at 6:00 this morning. I was to meet her at 9:00. Then, well, I was shot and then hit on the head, and whoever it was stole my car. Here's the good news. My car can be traced, so if whoever took her didn't ditch the vehicle, then we can locate her. My people are working on it, and I expect to hear back any moment. I have another idea that I want to run past you instead of us storming into the unknown."

"No way, Josh, Joe is an animal, and there is no telling what he will do to her. I want to get her the second you find out where she is."

"Jimmy," Bobby began, but my cell went off and I saw it was Joe, on video chat.

I answered and hit record. "Jimmy," Joe's ugly mug said, "I have something of yours." He held the phone in front of Theresa. Her face was black and blue, and her lip was bleeding. She was tied up and lying on her side. Joe grabbed her hair and held her face to the screen. "Say hi to your lover boy, sweetheart."

Theresa gazed at the screen. "Jimmy, I'm okay; don't do anything stupid."

Joe threw her head down and put the screen back on himself. "Yeah, Jimmy, don't do anything stupid. I will bring her to the meeting tomorrow with my pops. If everything goes according to plan, then she will be released. Try to come for her, and I will put a bullet in her head."

He hung up. Was he stupid? He'd just announced that he would put a bullet in the back of her head. "I got a recording of Joe threatening to shoot Theresa in the head. Can't we get him on that?" I demanded, handing my phone to Josh.

Bobby grabbed it and watched and sucked in his breath when he saw her face. "Bastard," he hissed. He shoved it in Josh's hands while he explained our situation.

"No, Jimmy," Josh spoke up. "If the other party doesn't know you're taping, it is considered illegal and won't be accepted in court, at least not in Philadelphia. What he said isn't enough, but add that to killing Christina, and we have a case."

"What? You got proof?"

Josh smiled. "I sure did. I checked the coroner's report, and then I checked the accident report. The cop who was first on the scene was an Italian kid, new to the force. I went over his report, and based on what he said, it didn't make sense. So, I went and talked to him. He'd been moved to another station just after the incident. I tried talking to him, but he said he couldn't remember the case. I went into evidence, and there was nothing logged. I took my chances and asked for the traffic cams from that day, at that intersection. It was sunset and a dry night. Christina's car was rear ended so hard, it hit the post, killing both on impact, but the driver of the car that hit them got out to check to make sure, and before he took off, the cam got a full view of his face. *It was Joe Mareno.*"

"Whew." I blew out my breath. "We got him then, on what, manslaughter?"

Josh nodded. "Add to that, the abduction of Theresa. There aren't web cams on the street I was on this morning, but my partner is canvassing the neighborhood, hoping for a witness who can verify that it was Joe who shot me. If that's the case, we can add aggravated assault with the intent to do bodily harm to a police officer to the list of charges, too."

"So, what now?" I asked. Standing here was killing me inside. Seeing Theresa's face all bruised and beaten, I would kill Joe when I got my hands on him.

"You have the meeting scheduled for tomorrow. All we know is that they have Theresa, and they will use her to enforce their claim. You will go to the meeting and act diplomatically, Jimmy, act as though you want nothing more than to cooperate. They will expect you to go alone, and you will. The police will stake out the place and have backup in all the hidden places. We have to stay out of sight. If they feel backed into a corner, they may just kill Theresa, and that is the last thing we want."

I sat down, suddenly feeling like I could no longer hold my own weight. Bobby came over with a glass of scotch. "Have some, Jimmy, it will take the edge off. Why don't you and Maggie stay here with us tonight; we have a guest room for her, and you can take the couch."

"Thanks, Bobby, but I know where I want to spend tonight. Listen, you know how to get ahold of me if there are any updates, and, Josh, I want to wear a wire."

"Jimmy, you can't; it's the first thing they will check for. Unless—the FBI has a new device, it's a lens that sits right inside your eye, like a contact. If we can get a hold of one and set you up before the meeting, that may work. Text me in the morning and tell me where you are. If I can get one, that will help us with the rescue."

I nodded, feeling suddenly exhausted. "I need to get my daughter. I have enough private security to make sure we are protected tonight. Thanks to you both for your help."

I took my leave. Before starting up my car, I texted Dean that I was on my way and needed his address.

He texted back. I put his address into GPS and shut my brain off while I drove. I wanted to pick up Maggie, now. Despite what Josh was hoping for, I didn't agree with his plan. I didn't trust Mareno to release her; a blood debt called for blood, didn't it?

There was only one person who knew what was going on, and the only way this could work was if I played dumb. I dialed Al while I drove.

"Hey, boss, what's up?"

"Hey, Al, Theresa was taken this morning by Joe. He sent me a live video of her, and she is beat up pretty bad."

Al was silent for a beat. "I'm sorry to hear it, boss. What's your plan?"

"I know where they're holding her, Al. I'm going to go and break her out."

"That sounds dangerous, boss. Want back up?"

"No, thanks, Al. Enough people have been hurt. I'll use my Jedi skills to sneak in and out before they know what hit them."

Before I'd left Josh and Bobby's, I saw the GPS report. I knew where she was, and it was in one of my own warehouses.

"I'll see you tomorrow, Al, at least I hope."

"Yeah, boss. Hey, what happened to Maggie today? She ditched cheerleading. Em couldn't find her anywhere, and she hasn't been answering her phone." I played stupid and said, "Really? Well, she did mention a guy named Dean to Theresa last night. She better not have snuck off with him." I put some steel in my voice.

"Oh, I'm sure it's nothing, boss. See you tomorrow, and be careful, Jimmy."

"You, too, Al."

I hung up the phone. Oh, he was good. He played me.

I texted Dean, asking if Mags could stay with him through dinner. He replied that it wouldn't be a problem. Good boy. I think I could like him.

I headed over to the warehouse, where Josh's car was said to be held. I watched; there was quite a lot of activity going on for the end of the day. The doors were open, and I saw Al talking to Joe. Sonofabitch! Joe patted him on the shoulder and then jumped in one of the company's cube vans. Theresa was in there; I knew it. When Joe had moved the phone from himself to Theresa, he showed me what I needed to know. I recognized the interior, just hadn't put it together. He was using my own company's resources to steal my girlfriend and keep her captive. I was furious.

I followed the van. It went into the underground parking of the hotel we were paying for him to stay in. I arrived at the bottom level in time to see Joe manhandling Theresa. He was trying to push her through a doorway. My girl was fighting, but she was tied at the wrists and ankles. Joe slapped her with such force that, even from this distance, I saw the blood spray from her nose.

Chapter 16

Theresa

I must have fallen asleep in the overly hot van, because the next thing I remembered was having my hair grabbed so hard, I yelped, and then a video chat was shoved in my face. It was Jimmy, and he looked murderous. If I were Joe Mareno, I'd be terrified.

I tried to assure Jimmy not to worry. His eyes told me everything; he would come for me, so when, hours later, the van pulled out, I got as ready as I could to fight whoever was driving it. It drove fast and squealed around several corners before coming to a stop.

Joe threw open the side doors and dragged me out. I used both my feet to kick at him and managed to knock him over more than once, before he managed to grab my hair and yank me to my feet. Winding up, he slapped me so hard, I saw stars and almost passed out.

He shoved me through a door and into a service elevator. He typed into his phone with one hand while he held me with the other. We took the elevator up to the kitchen. That must be how they brought up product from delivery vans to the kitchens. Who'd have thought I would be the delivery. I was hanging over Joe's shoulder, facing down. Every time I struggled, he'd slam his hand down on my ass and, finally, just left it there.

Ugh, he was disgusting. I was passing a wall when I suddenly saw shoes, and when I looked up, it was into the face of my beloved Jimmy. He held his finger to his lips. He held a frying pan in his hands and a knife in the other, making good use of the weapons only a kitchen could provide. I reached out and grabbed a wall, pulling me and Joe off balance.

I tumbled to the floor, and as Joe spun around to grab me, Jimmy slammed him in the face with the frying pan. He dropped it, scooped me up and ran like hell before any of Joe's people poured out from whatever crevices the cockroaches were hiding in and gave chase.

When we got to the parking lot, Jimmy got to the car and threw me in as someone came out the service door with a gun in his hand. "Duck, Theresa," Jimmy yelled as he jumped into the driver's seat and squealed up the ramp.

We heard shots ring out, and one hit the back corner of the car, but we got around and up to the ground level without any more incidents. Jimmy raced like a maniac across town to Bobby and Josh's, hefting me out of the car, and he ran up the two flights with me on his shoulder. When Bobby answered the door, he was shocked.

He certainly hadn't expected to see me trussed up like a Thanksgiving turkey. "Oh thank God," he said, shutting the door.

"Bobby, I need your keys. I have to get Maggie, in case they know where she is and go after her. Take care of T," Jimmy said. Then he raced back out with Bobby's keys.

Josh got on the phone, while Bobby cut the ropes binding my wrists and ankles.

"Copy that," Josh said and then hung up. With my hands loose, I threw my arms around Bobby and cried.

"Theresa, what did that animal do to you?" Bobby had tears in his eyes.

"Bobby, get the first aid kit, while I call an ambulance. I'll go with T; you stay here and wait for Jimmy."

"No." I'd finally found my voice. "I'm not going anywhere without Jimmy, not even to the hospital, Josh."

"Maybe you should forget the ambulance for now, Josh. What if they have someone on the inside and they get alerted?"

"You're right, Bobby. Between the two of us, we have enough medical training to fix the immediate problems. Theresa, did he hurt you anywhere else? Did he punch you in the stomach or—"

"No, Josh, he just wanted my face bashed up to provoke Jimmy. I think he wanted him to lose it and try to get me back. What happened?"

The guys shook their heads, and Bobby said, "We have no idea, Theresa. Last time we saw Jimmy was when he received the phone call from Joe. I don't know how he found you."

He went rummaging for the first aid kit then and came back with hot water, cloths, bandages and ointment. He wiped me down, disinfected the cuts—which hurt like hell—and then bandaged up a few cuts.

By then, Jimmy was at the door with Maggie. She saw me and burst into tears.

I held open my arms to her, and she ran into them. "It's okay, cara mia; I will be okay, I promise."

Then Jimmy moved Maggie and held me. "I'm so sorry, il mio amoré, please forgive me for letting this happen."

I clung to him and cried. Finally, the adrenaline wore off

and I was a mess. I wouldn't let him go; he had to carry me to the couch and sit down with me on his lap, my face buried in his neck. We must have fallen asleep, I realized, when I went to shift and there were arms around me. I opened my eyes and saw that I was still on Jimmy's lap on the couch. The lights were off, and everyone else had gone to bed.

"Jimmy?"

His eyes fluttered open; he looked utterly exhausted.

"Tesoro," he said with a smile. "How are you feeling?"

"Like I have been beaten with a bag of oranges. How bad does it look?"

His expression turned black. "Bad enough, bella, bad enough. Joe Junior and his crew have been arrested. I'm sure his father will post bail, if he can get it. Their attempts have failed, T, but just to make sure, I will keep my meeting with Joseph Mareno, Senior, tomorrow."

"But, Jimmy, why, what good can possibly come of a meeting with Mareno?"

"Theresa, just because we won this round doesn't mean the war is over. Josh has held back on the other charges, so far. All they and the police know is kidnapping. Not enough to keep Joe behind bars. I'm going to blackmail Joseph Mareno by having him sign a document that my lawyer has drawn up for me. The penalty for murder is execution. If Joseph wants to keep his son from lethal injection, he will accept my deal and move on."

I looked at him, shocked.

"I'm doing him a favor by removing his kid; he's a complete idiot. And, he will always owe me because, at any time, the evidence can be presented for attempted murder and double homicide, putting Joe on the chopping block. I have security measures in place, and if anything ever happens to me, then the evidence goes to the proper authorities. He can't touch me, besides, he won't want to. I'm selling him the company, and not for a dollar, as originally planned. If he wants it, he will pay full market value for it as I am holding all the cards. Then he can use it however he wishes."

I processed everything he'd just said. "But what will you do, you know, for work?"

"Don't worry about that, T. I'm rich and I did start my own little business on the side, a subsidiary of Falcone Property Development, that is all mine. Condo development, bringing up the value in previously underdeveloped areas of Philly. That is what Bobby's been helping me with. I'm going to offer him a position as senior executive of the design division."

I tried to smile, but it hurt my cracked lip and the movement made it bleed.

"I'm sorry, bella." He nuzzled against me, and I inhaled him, that masculine, woody, Italian coffee man smell that made me giddy.

Jimmy

My meeting with Mareno went exactly as planned. I took Josh with me, to verify all I said about the legalities of Joe's situation were fact. My lawyer was also in attendance to witness the signing of the contract.

Selling Falcone Property Development was easier than I'd anticipated. Mareno wanted it, and it went for a song. But I wasn't selling it for profit, although we made a tidy sum. It was an exchange, the last blood payment the Mareno family would ever extort from the Falcones.

Joe's life would always hang in the balance of any future decisions Joe, Sr. made. He sent Joe, Jr. back to Italy and left his daughter in charge of the newly acquired company, her second, Al.

I left Al out of everything, only Joe knew his involvement. He and I would never work together, and our friendship was over. Maggie could stay friends with Emma, but the days of sleepovers at their home was over. She wasn't allowed anywhere near their home. If a cheerleading practice or gig came their way, Theresa or I drove, or both of us.

I had a lot of free time these days, with not having to run such a monster of a business. I had a good enough reputation in the world of development that my projects were proving highly valuable, and I was doing more work I found interesting than being beholden to a limiting set of infrastructure I now felt was outdated.

Bobby and I were partnering with the city to help create safe but cheaply acquired dwellings for the homeless. My work, still successful, was now more rewarding.

It took several weeks for Theresa's face to fully heal. Luckily, she did not need stitches, so there were no scars to contend with.

One day, I was busy in my office when I heard a knock on the door.

"Come in."

Theresa opened the door, wearing the exact same outfit she'd worn when she came for my mother's wake. I stood up and strutted toward her, my look predatory. Her eyes shone with merriment. "Why, Theresa Romano, to what do I owe the pleasure?"

"Hi, Jimmy."

I indicated for her to sit in the same seat as before, and I stood in front of her, just inches away. "Can I help you with something, bella?"

"Um, well, I, uh."

"Theresa Romano, do you need some help getting that

tongue wagging?" I stood up and folded her over my desk. I pulled up her skin-tight skirt and landed two dozen stinging slaps to her gorgeous behind. She had filled out a bit in the past few weeks, no longer too skinny, and I, for one, was happy to see some meat somewhere besides her perfect ass.

I pulled her up and sat her on my knee at my desk. "Well?"

She grinned, her eyes all lit up. She had something important to share. "I remember now, Sir, here." Out of her black business jacket, she pulled a stick. I looked at it and saw a plus sign. "Congratulations, Jimmy, you're going to be a daddy again."

I was shocked, and suddenly wondered if spanking her, even in fun, was a bad idea.

She could see the direction of my thoughts. "Don't worry, I have a very liberal obstetrician whom Bobby recommended. I asked her already; spanking is fine."

I grinned and kissed her possessively, owning every reaction and moan that came from her beautiful mouth. "Theresa, my love, are you as excited as I am?"

She moaned "yes," into my mouth.

I hugged her and sat her back in her chair. "I was going to wait until the perfect moment, bella, but you have created it." I pulled open the drawer of my desk and pulled out a box, and getting down on one knee, I asked, "Theresa Romano, will you be my forever?"

Her eyes held unshed tears of happiness. "Yes, Jimmy, yes, I will be yours forever."

I took the two-carat blue diamond out of the box and slid it onto her finger.

"Oh, my goodness, Jimmy, it's beautiful."

"No, Tesoro, it pales in comparison to your beauty. I love you."

She smiled, her gaze filled with the trust and love she had

given me right from the beginning when we were just children. "I love you, too, Jimmy."

My heart filled, complete happiness descending over me like a mantle, and in that moment, I knew, no matter what curve balls life threw me, it would be a shadow in comparison to what I held in my hands, and I was grateful.

Skylar West

Skylar West is a Canadian writer, new on the author scene and making a big impact with her steamy romance books. She loves walks in the rain, hot cups of delicious java, overly large sweaters, and the type of steamy sex she writes about in her novels. A cat lover, this author looks forward to writing many more novels.

Find her on Facebook: https://www.facebook.com/sky.west.1806

Don't miss these exciting titles by Skylar West and Blushing Books!

Sons of Sicily series
His to Learn
His to Train

Crown and Cross series
Laughlin

Angels and Demons Series
Fallen Angel
Dark Angel Discovered
Dark Angel Awakened
Dark Angel Rescued
Dark Angel Redeemed

Single Titles

The Dark Side of Kingsley

Anthologies
12 Naughty Days of Christmas 2020

Blushing Books

Blushing Books is the oldest eBook publisher on the web. We've been running websites that publish steamy romance and erotica since 1999, and we have been selling eBooks since 2003. We have free and promotional offerings that change weekly, so please do visit us at http://www.blushingbooks.com/free.

Blushing Books Newsletter

Please join the Blushing Books newsletter
to receive updates & special promotional offers.
You can also join by using your mobile phone:
Just text BLUSHING to 22828.

Every month, one new sign up via text messaging will receive
a $25.00 Amazon gift card, so sign up today!